I0607957

TRIO

THREE SHORT STORIES

STEVIE TURNER

TRIO: THREE SHORT STORIES
Copyright © 2024 by STEVIE TURNER

All rights reserved. No part of this book may be reproduced or transmitted in any form or by any means without written permission from the author.

ISBN: 978-1-7394010-7-8

DEDICATION

For Phillip.

TABLE OF CONTENTS:

THE ART CLASS

CHAPTER ONE

He allowed the robe to slip over his shoulders and fall down where it pleased. Mark Richards angled his body slightly away from the artists, crossed his legs, and rested his head against a high-backed chair while allowing his dark fringe to hide both eyes. It was time to concentrate his thoughts on the fifty quid already tucked away in his wallet, which was not too bad for an hour's 'work' of looking as interesting and enigmatic as possible. However, even though the entrance was securely locked to dissuade interested spectators, the draughty Wybridge Institute was cold enough to freeze his balls off.

"Can we have a little more warmth please, maybe that heater that's above *me*?"

A murmur of assent travelled about the room. Out of the corner of his eye he saw one of the old biddies, Jean Bradley, put down her pencil and stand up.

"I'll turn the thermostat up straight away for you, Mark, although Mister Wainwright did stipulate the electric ceiling fires cost more money."

"Mister Wainwright can kiss my arse. *He's* not the one that's stark bollock naked, is he?"

"Thank God for that... he's eighteen stone at least." A new but definitely male voice spoke up from the back of the room. "I'll find out where the switches are for the overhead fires."

1970s central heating pipes creaked into life as the old woman, no doubt traumatised by his colourful use of language, returned to her seat. Mark risked a quick glance to his left to check out the new voice. A young man, no more than thirty, bleached and highlighted hair, had moved off towards what looked like a fuse box sited above the main entrance. Very soon, much to Mark's relief, warmth radiated down onto his body.

"Cheers, whoever you are."

"Paul Mercer, but don't look at my picture, okay?"

"Wouldn't dream of it, mate."

Mark basked in the heat as two clock hands on the wall opposite moved in agonising slowness from 7:30 to 8:30, while outside the February evening morphed from light rain to sleet. Not a soul uttered one single word as they sketched and erased, painted and primped their papers to perfection.

"Time's up." Mark shrugged into his robe and faced his audience. "See you again next week."

"Thanks, Mark." Jean waved her paintbrush in the air. "Sorry about the heating. I'll see if Mister Wainwright will let me unlock earlier next time so I can warm the place up a bit."

"And tell him we can't have Mark freezing his bits off." Paul grinned as he packed up his paints and easel. "Or there won't be anything left to draw."

"Appreciated."

Mark gave Paul a brief nod, then picked up his bag and made his way to the gentleman's lavatory to get dressed. He had time to don pants, trousers, socks and trainers before the door opened.

"With me being the only new bloke amongst all those old girls, I guess you're used to having this cubby hole to yourself on Monday nights." Paul strode towards the urinal. "Sorry… I'm dying for a piss."

"Be my guest." Mark threw on his tee shirt and jumper. "I'm done. Just got to find my car keys."

"You don't live locally then?"

"At Lydhouse. Me and my girlfriend rent a flat there."

Mark wrapped his coat more snugly around him, rummaged in his bag for some car keys, and then hurried out to where his Ford Mondeo sat covered in a thin layer of snow. Grateful for the engine starting first time, he increased the temperature to 25 degrees and pulled away from the kerb.

***

Turning his key in the lock, he opened the door and inhaled a pleasant scent of warm air coupled with a tang of roast chicken.

"How'd it go?" Marie appeared in the hallway.

"Same as usual." Mark planted a kiss on Marie's lips. "The old girls paid me a fiver each. Oh yeah, there's one bloke as well now. I sat there in the buff for an hour and thought about being in bed with you."

"You dirty devil. Don't think too hard about that otherwise they'll all have to adjust their pictures a bit."

"Huh, no chance. " Mark threw off his coat. "It's bloody cold in there for starters, and it's not as though there's any women in there under the age of seventy anyway."

"Pleased to hear it. By the way, my offer to clean the council offices twice a week has been accepted. Anything's better than picking bloody mushrooms. I can start in a fortnight. Tracy has just given in her notice."

"Oh, great. Hopefully we won't need to have two jobs each for much longer. Anyway, I'm starving." Mark gave Marie a squeeze. "Do I smell chicken?"

"You do indeed. Come and sit down. I've just got to make some gravy."

"Can I help dish up?"

"No, it's all done."

Mark took a seat at their small kitchen table and enjoyed the view of Marie's backside as she bustled about.

"Stop looking at my arse."

"It's a nice arse." Mark grinned. "Thank God the old biddies don't have to paint *mine*, because I sit on it."

"They're probably painting your willie instead."

"I keep my legs crossed. I don't think they can see it unless they stand in close and peer over."

"That reminds me… there's some chipolatas in the oven too, to go with the chicken." Marie put a heaped plate of food in front of Mark.

"Not one of those Cumberland sausages?"

"Definitely not."

"Shame." Mark attacked his meal with gusto. "I guess I'll have to make do with chipolatas instead then."

CHAPTER TWO

When he emerged from the Gents' toilets, Mark found many of the artists already seated and awaiting his arrival.

"Sorry I'm late, folks. I had to give my girlfriend a lift to her evening job. Her car wouldn't start."

"You're busy people." Andrea Gerrard opened her box of watercolours. "I was only saying the very same thing to Jean just now."

Mark noticed how Paul had moved from the back to the front row as he sat down, crossed his legs, and let his robe fall.

"Yeah, we're busy because our landlord has put up the rent. I'm not doing this because I'm an out and out exhibitionist, you know."

"You poor young people." Jean shook her head. "I don't know how you afford a place of your own these days."

"It's not even *ours*." Mark leaned against the back of his chair. "Finding a deposit for a mortgage is out of the question. I'll shut up now anyway, so that you can paint."

Silence ensued. He closed his eyes and tried to transport himself away from a feeling of uneasiness caused by an intense scrutiny of his body he felt that came mainly from behind the screen of Paul's easel. He'd been happy enough posing for the old girls, but there was something about the young man's gaze only a few feet away from him that rang a faint warning bell in his head.

It seemed as though four hours had passed instead of one. Mark, more than happy to push his arms through the sleeves of his robe again, stood up and tied the drawstring around his waist.

"I'm off then. See you all next time. How many more weeks do you want me for?"

"Another three should do it, and then we'll be back to fruit bowls I expect." Pat Oliver looked towards the other ladies, who nodded in assent.

"Okay." Mark picked up his bag and made his way out of the hall. "I'm off to get some clothes on."

On entering the gents' toilets he made his way to a cubicle, and then rammed the lock home when he heard the main door squeak.

"It's only me." Paul announced himself in a strident tone. "I need a piss."

"Carry on, mate."

Mark threw a jumper over his head and waited for the main door to squeak again. However, although now fully dressed, water still ran in the sink as Paul took an inordinate amount of time to wash his hands. Finally Mark gave up, picked up his bag, and opened the cubicle door.

"Fancy a pint in the pub next door?"

"Ah, no ta." Mark shook his head and made for the door. "My bird will have dinner ready."

"You don't like me much, do you?" Paul wiped his hands on a paper towel. "I'm receiving negative vibes again, coming from your direction."

"You must be imagining it, mate. I don't even know you. Anyway, got to go... see you next week."

"I'll be here." Paul's mouth gave a slight upward turn. "Paintbrush in hand."

Mark made a quick exit, grateful to join the throng of elderly ladies who stood and chatted in the foyer.

"Thanks again, Mark." Pat Oliver unlocked the main outer door. "I and all the others really appreciate it."

"I'm grateful for the extra money."

The night air, cold against his face, revived his good humour. In ten strides he reached his car and activated the central locking system. He threw his bag onto the passenger seat, then climbed in and locked the driver's door. In the rear view mirror he spotted Paul as he stood on the front steps of the Institute and stared in his direction. The bloke was definitely strange. Not even waiting to de-mist the front window, Mark rubbed his sleeve against the glass, started the engine, and drove away.

***

"I paid the rent today." Marie ran a cutter through a ham and mushroom pizza. "We're okay for another month."

"Great. Hopefully I'll be able to knock this evening job on the head soon and find something a bit better."

"You don't like it?"

"Not really. I think I'll see if there's any office cleaning *I* can do, or something like that."

"The old girls will be disappointed." Marie placed a plate of pizza, pasta and vegetables in front of Mark. "It's the end of the month. Couldn't afford any fillet steak."

"Ha, never mind, red meat is bad for you." Mark upended the tomato sauce bottle and added a splash of ketchup to his plate. "In fact, probably everything is, but hey… you're not."

"Glad to hear it." Marie sat down and picked up a knife and fork. "Maybe we can lie down and discuss this later on."

"I'm right there." Mark grinned. "Just let me finish my dinner first. By the way, how was work today?"

"Which one?"

"Oh yeah … the mushroom factory."

"Bloody awful. I had to have a shower as soon as I got in. I stank of mushrooms. You have to climb up on the mushroom beds, one leg on each bed, and there's all this steam coming at you from above."

"Hope the beds aren't too far apart."

"And then you have to cut the mushrooms while balancing on the beds."

"Sounds worse than *my* job. At least I get to sit down, do absolutely nothing and get paid for it."

"The beds are all slippery with the steam. One night I'm going to split my difference."

"That'll be interesting."

"Thank god I've only got another fortnight there."

"Yeah I know. I've only got another three weeks at the Institute, and then I'll find something else."

"How can we save up for a mortgage deposit if we're paying out all this money in rent?"

"Good question." Mark chewed thoughtfully on some pasta. "Win Euromillions?"

CHAPTER THREE

Mark gave a sigh. There he was again, standing on the steps of the Institute. Mark climbed out of his work's van and jumped down onto the pavement.

"Evening." Mark moved quickly past Paul towards the main door.

"It's locked." Paul turned to face him. "Nobody's here yet, just you and me."

"Well, I expect they'll all arrive in a minute."

"I'll wait in the van." Mark, unwilling to linger, retraced his steps.

"Can I join you? It's freezing tonight. Anyway, I thought you had a Mondeo, but I must admit to liking the '*Mark the Sparky*' inscription on the van. Yes, you can light my bulb any time."

"I do have the Mondeo, but it's iced up." Mark ignored the double entendre. "I've already used the van for work today, so it's not as bad."

He could already see Paul descending the steps. To his relief he saw Jean, Andrea and a few others approaching from a distance.

"Don't matter. I can see the old girls coming now."

Mark locked his van and waved at the group. Paul, noticeably disappointed, stopped in his tracks and headed back towards the Institute, stepping aside to let others through the door. Mark, closely followed by Paul, headed straight for the Gents' toilets and locked himself in a cubicle.

"Hey, you don't have to be bashful." Paul laughed. "You've got a great body. We're all boys together, yeah?"

"I feel uneasy with another bloke telling me I have a great body." Mark donned his robe and packed his clothes into a bag. "What I want you to do is to get out of my space."

Mark opened the cubicle door just in time to catch an icy stare from Paul, who turned on his heel, strode to the entrance, and slammed the door behind him. Satisfied that Paul had at last got the message, Mark sauntered into the hall and seated himself in his usual position on the stage.

"We're ready, Mark." Jean waved a paintbrush in the air.

Mark threw back his robe and crossed his legs, all the while conscious of Paul's stare.

"Don't cross your legs." Paul craned his neck around his easel. "We need to see your body properly."

"Fuck off." Mark closed his eyes and laid his head back on the chair. "Nobody else is complaining. I'll sit how I like."

"Okay, okay, don't get your knickers in a twist."

"He hasn't got any on." Andrea laughed. "Mark, you're doing great just as you are."

"Cheers."

He could usually let his mind wander for an hour while the old ladies painted away, but now with Paul Mercer almost drooling in front of him, Mark unsuccessfully tried to banish frequent waves of unease. When the session finished he collected his money then ran and locked himself in the disabled toilet to get dressed in private while everybody still chatted and packed away their easels and paints. He then hurried out of the Institute but stopped short at the sight of Paul, who stood by the van and stamped his feet in the snow.

"Where did you get to?"

"Getting dressed." Mark moved out into the road towards the driver's door and switched off the central locking, "In private."

"Would you be so kind as to give me a lift?" Paul opened the van's passenger door and slid in, throwing a gym bag onto the back seat. "It's black ice everywhere tonight, and I don't fancy carrying all my gear home in case I go arse over tit. I don't live far... just a few streets away. It'll take you two minutes."

"Why not bring your own car? I'm not a fucking taxi service."

"I'll pay you if you like." Paul slammed the passenger door shut. "Here... take this."

Mark caught a five pound note as it flew through the air.

"I don't want your money. I just want you to get out of my van."

"Oh, come on... I'm in here now. Take the fiver. Sycamore Street. Just go to the junction, turn right, and then it's first on the left. Number ninety two."

Mark inserted his key in the ignition, started and revved the engine, then screeched up to the junction. With tyres squealing in protest he made a right turn at speed, then threw the steering wheel around the first left hand turning and stamped on the brakes.

"There you are. Get out."

"My flat is at the other end. It's a long walk up this road."

"This is *it*, mate. If you don't get out I'm going to come round there and open the door, and then you'll wish you hadn't asked me for a lift."

"Okay, okay, I can take a hint."

"Please do." Mark sighed and drummed his fingers on the steering wheel. "And take your shit with you that's on the back seat."

"See you next week." Paul reached over for his bag. "When you're in a better mood."

***

Mark walked into the warmth of the flat, where a tantalising aroma of roast pork assailed his nostrils.

"Hey, babe, I'm home." He took off his coat and threw it at a coat hook.

"Dinner's ready!"

Mark made his way to the kitchen, kissed Marie on the cheek, then plonked himself down at the table."

"That's it. *Finito.* I'm not going back there."

"Why? What's happened?" Marie ladled gravy over two plates of pork, roast potatoes and vegetables. "It's good money, isn't it?"

"Yeah it is, but I don't want to talk about it. That dinner looks good. I'll get the local paper tomorrow after work and look for some evening cleaning jobs."

"Don't change the subject."

"Look… I just can't do it anymore. I don't *want* to do it anymore. Okay?"

"Okay." Marie put two heaped plates of food on the table. "You'd better tell the old girls then."

"I've got Jean's email addresses. I'll send her a message as soon as I've eaten." Mark speared a roast potato with his fork. "They'll have to use a bit of imagination to finish their pictures off. I'll work on the assumption that March is going to be a better month for me."

CHAPTER FOUR

It was fortunate that Marie had run out of soap powder, otherwise he would not have seen the notice in Lydhouse's shop window. Mark peered at the advert more closely:

'Wanted: Evening shop assistant to work here 7pm – 10pm weekdays. Pays national minimum wage.'

It would mean he would see even less of Marie in the evenings, but then again she would be out cleaning offices twice a week anyway. Mark opened the shop door, and the resulting tinkling bell brought Rita Horton scurrying towards the till.

"Hey, Rita." Mark raised one hand in greeting. "What about that advert outside? Have you found anybody yet?"

"Not yet. I've only just put it in." Rita shook her head. "I need to take evenings off. Ron complains he's like a widower."

"I can sympathise. Marie and I work during the day and then she's been picking mushrooms at night, but at the moment an evening job for me too would keep us out of the food bank. Our rent has just almost doubled. What I'm saying is... how about *me*?"

"Why not?" Rita laughed. "When do you want to start?"

"Shall we say tomorrow night? I'm still re-wiring The Grange, but it's an ongoing thing."

"Come in a bit earlier if you can, and I'll go over the till and other stuff with you. You won't need to worry about filling the shelves... I'll do that. You just have to serve the customers. I'll even come down at closing time, deal with the cash and lock up. Hey, it's a good thing I live over the shop."

"Or not, according to Ron." Mark pointed a finger towards the ceiling. "Oh, I'll take a box of soap powder now, and come back about six o'clock tomorrow."

"Great. No charge for the soap powder. It's on *me*. And Mark..."

"Yeah?"

"You can phone me at any time with a problem and I'll come down to help. I just need to give Ron a bit more attention."

"Ta. See you tomorrow."

***

It was money for old rope. Three customers all evening, although that might have been due to persistent heavy rain that ran in rivulets down the shop's front bay window. By nine thirty Mark had familiarised himself with the workings of the till and the layout of produce on the shelves, and had completed two crosswords he'd found in a stack of old newspapers. When Rita re-appeared on the dot of ten he found he was already looking forward to the following evening.

"Thanks Mark. You've done a grand job. Ron's not as mobile as he used to be, and he's getting more needy. He doesn't like being on his own, and he hates strangers talking to him if he comes down here."

"No problems. A total of twenty one pounds spent, but maybe things will pick up tomorrow if the rain stops."

"Oh yes, you can be sure of it. Sometimes I'm rushed off my feet. You're local, yeah?"

"Dinsdale Road, by the school."

"Great. Not far to walk then. See you tomorrow."

Mark pulled the collar of his jacket up around his ears and stepped out of the shop's womb-like warmth. Immediately a torrent of rain cascaded over his head and down the back of his neck. He made a dash for home, side-stepping puddles like Gene Kelly on steroids. By the time he turned a key in the lock there was no part of him that was dry. He stood dripping on the welcome mat.

"Shit."

"Is that *you*?" Marie ran out into the hallway. "Blimey, you'd better get those wet clothes off."

"I thought you'd never ask." Mark kicked off his trainers. "That's the best offer I've had all night."

"How'd it go?"

"A breeze. Three customers. I was bored to tears, but better than the last job." Mark divested himself of his jacket, jumper and wet jeans. "How about you?"

27

"Okay. I can categorically say that cleaning offices is better than picking mushrooms. You look quite sexy standing there in your socks and boxers though." Marie gave a wolf whistle through pursed lips. "I see the rain's soaked through. You'll have to get those pants off as well."

"If you insist." Mark put his arms around Marie. "Only if you do the same."

"Done."

***

Jean eventually replied to his email. Mark read how thankful they all were that he had given up his time, and how they looked forward to welcoming him back in the future. Mark decided only a very large pay rise would tempt him to take his clothes off in public again.

Shop work, dull as it was, had actually come in handy. Rita had given him extra hours and more responsibility after he had finished re-wiring the Grange Hotel, as his next electrical job was not due to start for a couple of weeks. One lunchtime in early April when few customers were about, Mark lifted a box containing bottles of fabric conditioner from the storeroom and carried it out to the shop. He put it down on the floor near an empty shelf, squatted on his haunches, and ripped open the top of the box.

"Come down a bit in the world then, have we?"

Mark turned his head in the direction of the voice and glanced up to find Paul Mercer towering over him and wearing a smirk.

"No. What makes you think *that*?"

"Oh, well... one day the famous male model, and now just filling shelves."

"What are *you* doing in here? I've never seen you in Lydhouse before."

"Just passing on my way to the gym and needed a sugar boost. If you've got the time, I'd like to pay for this bar of chocolate."

"There's no gym around here."

"What's this... a Spanish inquisition? I just want to pay for a fucking bar of chocolate."

"There's a self-service till by the window."

"I tried it. It doesn't work. You'll have to show me what I'm doing wrong."

With some reluctance Mark stood up and made his way to the normal till, pleased to be able to close a security gate behind him.

"Just give it here, and I'll scan it." Mark held out his hand for the chocolate. "I'll report the self-service one to the owner."

"Why haven't you been turning up at the Institute?" Paul placed the chocolate bar in Mark's hand. "We've all missed you."

"Got better things to do with my time. That's one pound twenty five pence please."

"Shame. D'you want to see my picture of you?"

"Not really." Mark scanned the chocolate wrapper and shook his head. "Especially if you've made my dick twelve foot long."

"You wish! You should see what I've done. I'll bring the picture in tomorrow."

"Please don't." Mark took the coins and handed back the chocolate bar. "Just forget it."

Paul took the chocolate and made his way out of the shop. Mark filled the rest of the shelf with bottles of conditioner, his good mood evaporated.

CHAPTER FIVE

"Leave the breakfast stuff in the sink. You get off to the office. I'll wash up." Mark stood up from the table carrying his dirty plate. "I've got plenty of time."

"You're not working?" Marie turned to Mark with a quizzical expression on her face. "Rita doesn't want you?"

"I'm not going to the shop today. I've got a couple of quotes to do for fire alarm installations."

"How about tonight?"

"No." Mark shook his head. "I've told Rita I'm not going in until tomorrow."

"Oh well, okay. I'll see you later." Marie came towards him. "Give us a kiss."

"Yeah, I can do that." Mark laughed, put his arms around Marie and planted a kiss on her lips. "That's well easy."

"Love you, Mark."

"Love you too."

The flat suddenly felt empty without her. Mark washed the breakfast crockery and put it away. The quotes he needed to do would not take long, and the rest of the day stretched out like an endless ribbon. He was in two minds about whether to change his plans and give Rita a hand, but then again a day off felt more appropriate.

After a leisurely bath, a quick glance through the front net curtains showed a quiet street, with nobody about in the weak sunshine. Mark donned his Kevlar jacket and trousers, shrugged his shoulders into a rucksack, slipped his hands into gauntlets, and stuffed his feet into leather motorbike boots. He put a crash helmet over his head, then let himself out of the flat and walked down the main staircase and around to the back road where his bike stood under a makeshift awning. He unlocked the security chain, and then with just one turn of the ignition key the bike roared into life.

He had already been recognised by foreman Dave Parsons at the new build nursing home in Wybridge as he pulled up at the entrance. Mark waved a gauntlet at Dave, then rode the bike to a less muddier place to park. He took off his crash helmet and shook his head.

"That's a mean old machine. You sold the Mondeo?" Dave walked up to the bike and gave it an approving nod. "You come for the fire quote?"

"The Mondeo's outside the flat, and I've still got the work's van too. Thanks for putting in a good word for me."

"One good turn deserves another. You helped me out at short notice."

"Pleasure. I'll have a look around, take some measurements, and then send you a text."

"Fancy a pint at lunchtime? The Wybridge Arms?"

"How about '*The Dog*' at Lydhouse?" Mark walked with Dave towards the front door of the nursing home. "They do a mean steak and kidney pie."

"You're on. See you there. One o'clock."

***

A pleasantly warm rush of air hit his face as Mark pushed open the door of the public bar. Dave had already taken a seat on one of the bar stools, and raised one hand in greeting.

"I've ordered the first round, and two pie and chips."

"Cheers." Mark took off his jacket and sat down next to Dave. "I'll get the next round in."

The pub was unusually quiet for the time of day. Dave took two pints of beer from the landlord and slid one in Mark's direction.

"How's it going?"

"Not too bad. Could do with a bit more work, but I've got a couple of re-wire jobs coming up next month, plus the nursing home's fire alarm system when you give me the go-ahead."

"Marie okay?"

"So far so good." Mark took a long swig of beer. "She still works at the council offices, but now she's managed to get an evening job cleaning there as well."

"Good for her."

The landlord brought out two oval plates piled high. Mark picked up a knife and fork from a nearby holder.

"Marie would have something to say about all this cholesterol."

"Women do. Shirley's the same. By the way, talking about women, my mother-in-law lives in Lydhouse."

"Yeah?" Mark chewed on a chip. "Whereabouts?"

"Near the shop. She goes to the art class at Wybridge Institute. She and Shirl were looking through some photos and came across that one Shirley took of us two pissing about on Cromer beach. She recognised you and said you've been posing in the buff for them to paint."

"She's talking out of her arse." Mark laughed. "She must have got me mixed up with somebody else."

"I told her exactly the same. I said I'd known you since school and *that* would be the last thing you'd ever do."

Dave's outburst had taken the edge off his appetite. Mark gave his attention to the pie and eschewed the pile of chips.

"She's probably seen me in Lydhouse's shop. I work evenings there."

"Ah, yeah, that'll be it. I'll tell her if she mentions it again."

"*Do*. I told you they make a great pie here, didn't I?"

"Yeah."

CHAPTER SIX

"Hi Rita, hope it wasn't too busy for you yesterday." Mark closed the shop door behind him. "Where d'you want me to start?"

"There's a sack of potatoes you can get from the store room if you like, along with a few bags of carrots and onions. The veggie section needs filling."

"Okay, I'm on it."

"Oh, and Mark…" Rita stood up from pricing some cans. "Some bloke came in the shop yesterday looking for you."

"Bleached hair? About five foot ten?"

"That's it. He was carrying something flat in a case, like a picture maybe. I told him you weren't working. He asked me where you lived."

"What did you tell him?" Mark tried to ignore a sudden sinking feeling in his stomach.

"I said Dinsdale Road, but that I didn't know which number. Did he find you?"

"I was out yesterday, so I haven't seen him. I'm sure he'll turn up again soon."

"I'll leave you to get on with it now. Ron's not feeling too well today, so I need to be upstairs with him."

In the store room, Mark's ears were tuned to the entry bell's tinkle, but there were still no customers by the time he had filled the vegetable trays. He spent the whole afternoon on tenterhooks, but had relaxed by the end of the day after Paul failed to arrive. When Rita took over, Mark left the shop and enjoyed a brief walk home in unusually spring-like weather.

"Hi!" Mark turned his key in the lock. "I'm back!"

He smiled at Marie as she rushed towards him in the hallway.

"There's a bloke in the front room." Marie stood on tiptoe to hiss into Mark's ear. "I came home from work and he was walking up and down the street. He asked me where you lived. I said I was your girlfriend and he told me he had a gift for you. He followed me in and asked if he could wait until you came home."

"Fuck. That's it!." Mark threw his jacket at one of the coat hooks. "I've had enough!"

"Who is he? Why does he want to give you a gift?" Marie, perplexed, stared at Mark.

"I don't know, but don't worry, I'll get rid of him. Go and wait in the bedroom." Mark strode towards the living area. "He won't be coming back here again, I can assure you."

Mark ran to the living room and threw open the door, causing one brief moment of satisfaction as Paul jumped up in alarm.

"Fuck off *now*! If you don't go, I'm going to chuck you out. I don't want you bothering me or my girlfriend anymore. You come round here again and you'll get a kicking." Mark waved one arm towards the door. "Out!"

"Okay, okay, I'm going…" Paul shrugged and moved rapidly past Mark. "I only wanted to give you the picture I painted."

"Stick it up your arse."

Mark beat Paul to the front door, opened it wide, and then slammed it as Paul beat a hasty retreat. Marie came out of the bedroom and into the hallway.

"Can you please tell me what's going on?"

"Some sicko from the art class won't leave me alone."

"You've got an admirer?" Marie burst out laughing. "Am I hearing this right?"

"Don't take the piss, Marie, that's all I need."

"But doesn't he realise you're not gay?"

"I've given him enough clues, but he won't take *no* for an answer. If you see him hanging around again, phone me straight away. I think I'll have to get the police involved next time."

"He seemed like a nice guy though."

"I've told him to stay away. Nice guy or not, I don't want him round here."

Mark locked the front door and walked back into the living room with one arm around Marie's shoulders.

"Switch the TV on. I'll just go to the fridge and grab a beer, then we can find a film to watch."

Mark returned to the living room with a can of lager in one hand, and some hot cross buns in the other.

"Easter's come early, hasn't it?"

"Mark... look..." Marie lifted up a flat carryall. "He's left *this* down by the side of the settee."

"Oh, shit." Mark shook his head in disbelief. "Don't undo the bag. I don't want to see what he's done. It's going straight outside in the bin."

Mark put the can and hot cross buns down on the coffee table, then took the carryall from Marie, folded it in half, and stamped on it. He then folded it into quarters, put it on the floor, and let his weight flatten the carryall down further.

"I'll take it to the recycling bin, Mark." Marie bent down and picked up the bag. "I'll call on old Mrs Wentworth at number four at the same time. She said she needs a couple of things from the shop. Have a look on the Firestick to see if there's any nice documentaries. I don't want to watch animals getting killed and eaten though. Back in a minute."

Mark sat down, took a hot cross bun from the packet, and flipped the ring on a can of lager. He ate the bun, glugged a good part of the beer, then put his feet up on the coffee table and rested his head against the back of the settee.

CHAPTER SEVEN

He awoke to a programme on TV that he did not recognise. He rubbed his eyes, checked his phone, and was surprised to see how six hours had passed seemingly in an instant. He felt hungry. Scant light came through the window from the street lamp outside, and in the darkness he saw no sign of Marie. Mark stood up, yawned, and turned off the television. He thought it unusual that Marie had not woken him up at dinner time and had taken herself off to bed instead. However, he had been tired, and perhaps she had decided it was best to let him sleep.

He went into the kitchen, but no dinner had been left out for him to microwave. Mark popped some bread into the toaster, and heated up a can of beans. Satisfied with his perfunctory meal, he turned off the kitchen light, had a quick shower, and then crept naked into the bedroom.

The first thing that hit him was how the bed had not been slept in. Mark, confused, switched on a bedside lamp to make sure, then whirled back into the hallway and made a quick check of the other five rooms. *Where was Marie at this time of night?* He was now the only person in the flat.

The central heating had long ago turned itself off, and cold air had caused his skin to form goosebumps. Mark donned clean jeans, a warm jumper and trainers, then picked up a set of keys and a torch, let himself out of the flat, then lifted the latch on the door to the refuse/recycling area where three communal rubbish bins stood like sentinels in the night. The area appeared empty. Mark checked inside the bins but could not see the carryall bag that Marie had supposedly thrown away, although there was plenty of other rubbish piled up. Worried now, he closed the lids and shouted.

"Marie?"

His voice had a definite echo to it. Somewhere nearby an owl hooted. Mark hurried around the entire circumference of the block of flats, but arrived back where he started still none the wiser. He ran back to the flat, grabbed his phone, and pressed the last number he had called. A buzzing sound from behind made him spin around, where Marie's phone vibrated on the settee. He took a sip from the half-empty can of lager to offset a sudden dry mouth, and dialled 999.

"Emergency Services. Fire, police or ambulance?"

"Police. Police. My girlfriend is missing."

"Please give me your contact details and I will forward this call for you."

"Police. Detective Sergeant Mike Lewis. " A male voice rumbled in his ear almost instantaneously. "Please can you state your problem?"

"My girlfriend has disappeared." Mark tried to stop his voice rising in panic. "She's gone."

"Have you had an argument?"

"No. Nothing like that. She went out to take something to the rubbish bin and never came back."

"She might have met up with a friend."

"It's two o'clock in the morning! She went outside over six hours ago."

"Why didn't you ring six hours ago?"

"I fell asleep. Are you going to help me?"

"We'll send an officer round later on today if she hasn't returned. Let us know. I'll give you the number to call. Your girlfriend is probably staying overnight with a friend."

"No, she isn't!" Mark kicked the side of the armchair. "I've just told you she's missing!"

"And I've told you she'll probably turn up later on. We will act if there's no sign of her after twenty four hours. You've no idea of the number of responsible adults that just decide to take a rain check every now and then. We cannot send officers out on every single call we receive... there's just not enough of us go to around."

"Give me your number, and I'll let you know." Mark closed his eyes and took a deep breath. "Expect to hear from me very soon."

***

It was impossible to relax while Marie's whereabouts were unknown. Mark banished thoughts of any further sleep, locked the flat, then ran out to his car and started the engine. Without a firm destination in mind he drove from street to street, keeping watch for a red-haired woman, in fact *any* red-haired woman, just in case. By 05:30 tired, hungry and distraught, he returned home, parked the car and ran straight to the bedroom where again he found it empty. He flopped fully dressed upon the bed while his mind roamed back to the last moments he'd had with Marie.

The picture. She had gone to dump Paul's picture, and now it had disappeared, along with Marie. *Could there be a connection?* In his mad rush to start searching he had entirely omitted to drive along Sycamore Street in Wybridge, where he had once dropped Paul off on that icy February night not too long ago. Satisfied, Mark closed his eyes.

Birdsong woke him up from a fitful sleep. After a shower and shave, Mark grabbed his car keys and opened the door to the flat. Down by the main entrance mat he bent down to pick up an envelope. He turned it over, read his name, then ripped it open.

'Don't bother involving the police. Marie is with me at 92 Sycamore Street, Wybridge. I don't need any money, but I have a proposal I want you to agree to. I'm willing to meet you

at five thirty this afternoon outside the Institute. Don't try anything funny, because three of my friends will be with Marie while we meet up. Paul.'

Mark checked his watch and then punched the main door, which clattered in shock. Behind him he could hear that old Mrs Wentworth had ventured out into the foyer.

"Is everything all right?"

"Fine." Mark nodded. "No worries."

He still had eight and a quarter hours to go.

***

He saw Paul already there pacing up and down outside the Institute, while two heavies sat on the steps to watch and wait. Mark cut the car's engine and jumped out onto the pavement. Immediately both heavies stood up and strode towards him, with Paul in front. Mark took a deep breath.

"You *bastard*. Where's Marie?"

"I told you... she's at my house with three of my friends."

"If they touch one hair on her head, I'll kill you."

"Relax. They're not interested in *her*, and nor am I. It's *you* I want to speak to."

"I'm not listening to any proposals until I speak to Marie."

"Okay, okay, have it your way." Paul took a phone from his pocket and tapped in a number. "Rog, he wants to talk to her. Put her on."

Mark took the phone from Paul and held it against his ear.

"Marie?"

"Oh, Mark…"

"Are you all right?"

"They haven't touched me, if that's what you mean. I've had food and drink. It's just that I can't leave."

"I'm sorting it *now*. Hang on and I'll be there soon after I've spoken to Paul."

The call ended abruptly. Mark handed the phone back and glanced with envy at people as they drove home from work or walked about the village going about their daily business.

"So… *speak*. Tell Gert and Daisy to piss off back to the steps."

"Go on." Paul turned to the two men and waved one arm in the direction of the Institute. "Wait over there."

"Get it over with before I punch the daylights out of you." Mark instinctively clenched both fists. "What the fuck do you want?"

"*You*, darling. I want y*ou*. I *love* you. I've loved you from the first moment I saw you sitting naked in that chair. Agree to one night with me, *tonight*, and I'll let your girlfriend go. I'm clean, I'm healthy, and you won't catch anything nasty. I'll get some friends to film us of course, for me to look at for years to come, but if you go to the police afterwards I'll share our one night of passion all over social media."

"I'm not your darling for a start, and you're out of your tiny mind." Mark shook his head. "I don't have sex with men. I only took the job to earn a bit more money. The thought of being in bed with you makes me want to vomit."

"I *know* that, which is why I need some insurance." Paul sighed. "My friends have Marie. I'm giving you one option, and one option only, and that is one night with me, in *your* bed, in order to get her back. I won't bother you any more after this. You have my word. Of course Gert and Daisy will be with us, just in case you...er... get carried away. They like to watch. We'll go to your flat now, so you don't have a chance to go to the police. You never know... you might even like it. I've never had any complaints before."

"Don't bank on it, and I already went to the police yesterday." Mark hissed through clenched teeth.

"Tell them she returned home. Tell them anything you like, except the truth. Don't forget... my friends have Marie." Paul waggled one finger in Mark's direction. "Do it *now* and don't make it harder for her. In this way we can both get what we want. She will return to you as soon as I get back home in one piece tomorrow morning."

Mark searched his phone contacts for Sergeant Lewis's number, all the while trying in vain to think of a way out of the situation. He came to the conclusion there was none.

CHAPTER EIGHT

He'd had two showers, but two wasn't enough. By the time Marie walked in through the door he'd had two more. Mark, still damp and wearing a dressing gown, hurried to the hallway and put his arms around her.

"So glad you're home, baby."

He slammed the door shut with one foot and held her until her tears subsided.

"What did they do to you?"

"Nothing, apart from when they bundled me into their car." Marie's voice came in short gasps. "I really can't complain, except I wasn't allowed to leave until this morning. They even apologised and gave me a lift home. *Why did they do it?* They'd put that picture of you on the wall that Paul had painted, and even though you'd damaged it I could tell it was really very good. Are you going to the police?"

"I phoned them yesterday and they said to wait 24 hours in case you turn up. Anyway, it's over now. You turned up. I've sorted it. They won't bother us again."

"But they kidnapped me!" Marie stepped back and looked at Mark. "How can you leave it like that?"

"I gave Paul what he wanted, but I don't need to go into details. As I said, there won't be a repeat. It's over. All we have to do now is get on with our lives."

"But what did you have to do?"

"Nothing that's going to affect *us*. Come on, let's have something to eat. I haven't been able to eat properly since you've been gone."

With one arm around her shoulders, Mark led Marie along the hallway.

"What about a fry up? There's bacon, sausages and eggs in the fridge. We've got baked beans and bread. What more do we need?"

"I'm not hungry." Marie shook her head. "I just want to soak in a bath."

"You'll have to wait a bit for the hot water. There's none left."

"You've taken it all? Why? You only usually have a quick shower. We can't afford for you to fill the bath right up to the top every time you want to have a wash."

"Sorry." Mark held up his hands in supplication. "It won't happen again."

"I couldn't sleep, Mark. In fact, I'm knackered. I think I'll have a nap before anything else. Do you want to come and lie down with me?"

"The sheets and pillowcases are in the washing machine, but we can quickly find spares and make the bed again."

"*I've* been kidnapped and all *you* do is take the hot water and change the sheets? Did you do the hoovering and dusting as well? Bake a cake?"

"No. I went out looking for *you* until the early hours. Then I came back and ripped off the bedclothes because I could still smell your perfume on the pillows when I tried to sleep, which was doing my head in. I laid down on the settee, and no… surprise surprise, I didn't sleep *there* either."

"Sorry. I'm just tired."

"Yeah, well… so am I."

"Mark, let's forget about this conversation, go to sleep for a couple of hours, and then we can start again."

***

He awoke with a start, disorientated. He checked the digital clock, which read 15:39. With Marie still sleeping by his side, Mark climbed carefully out of bed and padded along to the kitchen. He returned with two cups of coffee and a plate of biscuits to find Marie awake and rubbing her eyes.

"The noise of the kettle woke me up."

"Sorry, but unless we get going we'll never sleep tonight. It's going on four o'clock in the afternoon. Have this coffee first though." Mark walked around to Marie's side of the bed and sat down on the edge of the mattress. "I thought you weren't going to buy any more chocolate digestives."

"Thanks." Marie took a steaming cup. "I wasn't but they're your favourites. By the way, I can think of something we can do to get going in a minute."

"The same thing *I'm* thinking about?"

"Yeah." Marie laughed. "Wait 'til I've had my coffee first though."

Anticipation of the sexual act had usually ensured an immediate erection in the past. However, even though he sipped his coffee slowly and nibbled away at most of the biscuits, by the time Marie pulled him closer his usual reaction had failed to materialise. Mark, dismayed beyond belief, mentally conjured up a plethora of pornographic pictures he'd implanted in his long term memory since the age of about thirteen.

"Sorry. For some reason it's not happening today."

"It doesn't matter." Marie kissed him. "There'll be other times and other ways. Just lie on top of me for now. It's nice."

Mark closed his eyes and let his body relax, while Marie wriggled beneath him, her legs wrapped around his back. For some unknown reason he wanted to cry.

CHAPTER NINE

Again, Mark had found himself seated at the bar of '*The Dog*' at closing time, not as inebriated as on the first night, but oiled enough not to mind Marie's searching questions on his return home. After the second bell, he gulped down the rest of his beer and stood up.

"See you tomorrow, Ray."

A cold wind hit him in the face as soon as he stepped out into the street. It was but a short walk to the block of twelve apartments, but as he rounded the corner into Dinsdale Road he could see his own flat still illuminated. He let himself into the hallway as quietly as he could.

"Bad luck. I didn't go to bed and leave the lights on." Marie, clad in pyjamas and dressing gown, padded out to meet him. "Pissed again?"

"I may be a lot of things, but pissed I'm *not*." Mark lurched towards the rack of coat hooks and threw his jacket onto the first one. "I'm going to have a shower and then go to bed."

"You stink of alcohol. I'm spending the night on the sofa."

"Do what you like." Mark shrugged. "It's a free country."

Pleasantly sleepy after a hot shower, Mark peeped into the front room. Marie's soft snores filled him with relief.

***

"How much longer are you going to waste our hard-earned money in the pub every night?" Marie slid a plate of bacon, egg, hash browns and beans in his direction. "Or is it *me* you're trying to avoid?"

"Why d'you say that?" Mark picked up a knife and fork. "I like spending time with you."

"Well, colour me stupid, but for the last fortnight you've come home from work, eaten your dinner, and then either gone to the shop or to the pub until closing time. You haven't invited me to go with you, and also we haven't had sex for over two weeks, which is strange in itself. I've got to ask... are you seeing somebody else?"

"No, I'm not." Mark toyed with a piece of bacon. "I've told you before and I'll tell you again... I love you very much. Leave me be... I can't be doing with all this drama."

"Then *speak* to me for God's sake and tell me what it is I've done to upset you."

Mark, his appetite gone, slammed down his cutlery and stood up.

"You haven't done anything wrong, except to keep going on and on at me. I'm going to work, and if you don't shut up with your bloody nagging I'll go to the pub again after dinner."

"You best do that." Marie shoved some bacon into a bun and took a large bite. "Because there won't *be* any dinner. I've checked the bank account. Payday isn't until next week, and you've drunk the rest of this month's housekeeping money away. I'm having a cheese sandwich this evening, and there's nothing left for *you*."

"Put this breakfast in the fridge then, and I'll have it tonight."

"Do it yourself."

Mark picked up his plate of food and hurled it at the refrigerator. Shards from the broken plate mixed in with egg yolk and bean juice dripped down the door and onto the carpet.

"Whoops, I missed."

"Go fuck yourself, Mark. You might like that. Hey, you don't seem able to fuck anybody else, do you?"

His hands balled into fists as he strode out of the kitchen. He grabbed his car keys, threw open the front door, then ran outside and slammed it behind him as hard as he could.

***

"Hi Rita… instead of paying me later on, d'you think I could take tonight's wages in food instead?"

Within an instant her puzzled expression had changed to one of concern.

"Oh… well, yes of course, if you're short." Rita nodded. "What would you like?"

"Maybe a couple of those Cornish pasties we can heat up in the microwave and some yoghurts? A loaf of bread, some milk and some fruit?"

"Help yourself, Mark. I'm happy for you to take what you need."

"Thanks. A couple of customers have paid me, but the cheques will take another day or so to clear, and Marie doesn't get her wages until next Friday."

"I know how you young folks struggle these days. It was bad enough when Ron and I were starting out, but you have it worse now. Just call me and I'll check it out for stocktaking before you go. The till automatically does it, you see, but I won't put your stuff through that way."

"I will, cheers."

***

The flat was in darkness as he approached the main door. Mark, bag of groceries in one hand, tapped in the entry code and ran up the single flight of steps to his apartment. He flicked on the fluorescent kitchen light, which spluttered to life to reveal a note propped up against a vase of daffodils on the kitchen table.

'I've gone to stay with my parents for a while until you've sorted yourself out. Let me know. Marie.'

There were none of her usual long rows of kisses. Remains of his smashed breakfast plate plus congealed egg, beans and bacon, still lay on the floor by the fridge. He cleaned up the mess, then ate two Cornish pasties, three slices of bread and two yoghurts. When he checked his phone messages there was a go-ahead for the fire alarm system at Wybridge Nursing Home from Dave, but nothing at all from Marie.

CHAPTER TEN

He was reluctant to venture into Wybridge again so soon, but his quote had been accepted and two weeks of solid work could not be turned down. Mark loaded his Transit van with tools, ladders and cables, then locked the flat and drove the few miles to where a brand-new nursing home stuck out from the surrounding buildings like a sore thumb. He left the van outside in a visitor's space and entered the front door, where an aroma of wood shavings and gloss paint assailed his nostrils. A man wearing grubby white overalls and carrying a pot of paint gave him a nod.

"You're the sparky, yeah?"

"That's me." Mark lifted his bag of tools in greeting. "I'll just let Dave know I'm here."

"He's upstairs. Something's wrong with the plumbing in one of the bedrooms."

Mark took the stairs two at a time and followed the sound of voices to where Dave and a plumbing sub-contractor wrestled with copper pipes in one of the en-suite bathrooms.

"Dave... just letting you know I'm now starting on the fire alarm system." Mark stuck his head around the door. "Be about two to two and a half weeks."

"Great. Me and a couple of the subbies meet down *The Wybridge Arms* for a pie and a pint or ten every lunchtime around half past twelve."

"I'll do my best." Mark chuckled. "Too many pints and electrics don't go well together."

"No excuses… you're buying the first round, you wanker. Two pints of lager and a Guinness."

***

With some reluctance, Mark pushed open the door to *The Wybridge Arms* at twelve thirty five. He made a quick scope of the public bar, where to his relief just a small group of men of pensionable age played cards and sat drinking in one corner. Dave and two other contractors sat on barstools and leaned against the counter.

"You're late." Dave raised the middle finger of his right hand in Mark's direction. "I've got the first round in. Still IPA, right?"

"Ta." Mark nodded. "I'm a bit short until next week, but I'll get the pies."

After ordering four steak pies, Mark tucked himself away at the end of the counter facing the door. He made idle chit-chat, declined any further beer, and ate mechanically, checking out each new customer as they entered. After he had drained the dregs from his glass he stood up and wiped the last crumb from his mouth.

"Got to get back… there's some cables dangling."

"But they're not connected, right?" Dave laughed and took a swig of beer.

"Well… no… but I've left some ladders about as well, and my drill and circular saw. I don't want them going walkabout. Thanks for the pint though."

"See you later."

Mark made his way outside and then hurried along the pavement towards the nursing home, making a mental note to investigate a parking space for the van somewhere around the back and more out of sight.

***

It had been a good day's work… the kind where nothing major had gone wrong. Whistling, Mark picked up his bag of tools and shouted along the corridor to where Dave, clipboard in hand, was in the process of signing a sudden flurry of timesheets.

"I'm off. See you tomorrow."

"Yeah, I'll sign you out, Mark. Give my regards to Marie."

At least the days were now longer with the start of May. Mark, grateful for slightly warmer weather, unlocked the back of his van, threw his tools inside, then secured the padlock and walked around to the driver's door. A fluttering of paper under the windscreen wiper stopped him in his tracks. With a sinking feeling of trepidation gnawing at his innards he lifted the note, then hopped into the van to read it in private:

'Hi, I was literally just passing and saw your van. I miss you. We had fun that night, didn't we? I've left my mobile number below if you ever want to get in touch.'

Mark screwed the paper up into a tight little ball and flung it over his shoulder into the depths of the cables, chisels, cutters and extension leads.

***

Still no beep of an answerphone message or letter from Marie. Mark checked the post once again, then closed the front door and locked it. Before his shower he tapped onto Marie's contact details and tried to call, but again heard the usual 'unavailable' message. He cobbled together a pile of cheese and tomato sandwiches, and spent the evening staring unseeingly at the TV screen.

CHAPTER ELEVEN

"You're quiet." Dave bit into a chicken pie.

"Oh, no reason." Mark shrugged. "Just thinking about the best way to run the cables to that smoke detector in the conservatory."

"Chill out. It's lunch time. I've got a spare ticket for the footy on Saturday if you want it?"

"Sounds good." Mark nodded. "Cheers."

"Marie won't mind?"

"She's staying with her parents at the moment." Out of the corner of his eye Mark checked the newcomer through the door. "Oh, fuck."

"What? You two not getting on?"

"There's someone just come in who I don't want to see."

"Too late... he's coming straight towards you."

Mark kept his gaze down upon the plate of pie and chips in front of him and ate in silence.

"Hi. Didn't know you would be in my local."

"Piss off, Paul." Mark chewed on a chip.

"Well, that's nice, I must say."

"He said *piss off*." Dave waved one hand in the direction of the door. "So...off you go then."

About to reply but then thinking better of it, Paul turned away in the direction of the bar.

"Who's that fucking poofter?" Dave glugged the rest of his beer. "What did he want with *you*?"

"Christ knows." Mark watched Paul's retreating back and grinned. "I think he's a friend of Marie's. Anyway, I'll head on back now and sort out my cables. See you later."

Mark stood up and strode towards the door, resisting the urge to look back. Once outside he enjoyed the early summer sunshine on his face as he made his way back to the nursing home.

"Just wait, you fucker. Let me catch up." Paul panted. "Don't keep hurrying away."

Mark turned and swung his fist in an effort to connect with Paul's nose.

"You've got to be quicker than that." Paul ducked. "Who's that guy you were with? Your boyfriend?"

"Yeah, we're getting married in July." Mark kicked out at Paul's shin. "He's very possessive, and so I'd keep away if I were you."

"Well, you're not me, and I can do what I like. I *know* you want *me*. I watch that video every day, and I can tell. It only took one night, but you liked it, didn't you?"

"No, I didn't. The next time you come anywhere near me I'm going to the police."

"You've got my phone number. Ring me." Paul jumped back to avoid another kick. "Be true to yourself. Life's better that way."

Mark ran up the path to the nursing home and looked over his shoulder. To his dismay, behind Paul he saw Dave in the distance as he rounded the corner from the pub. "Go fuck yourself, Paul, or whoever else you want to, but leave me the hell alone if you don't want to get arrested."

***

He felt at one with the crowd as they roared their displeasure at the referee's decision and questioned his parentage. Mark shouted the odds just for the sake of it, and enjoyed a great release of tension that had built up over the previous fortnight.

"Thanks for the ticket, Dave. Let's hope they win on penalties."

"No probs. Fancy a pint after the game?"

"You're on."

The stand erupted as the ball sped past the goalkeeper and into the back of the net, drowning out the final whistle. Mark playfully punched Dave's arm and yelled as loudly as he could.

"U. Nite. Ed!"

"Come on. Let's get to the bar before this mob does." Dave pushed past two United supporters to reach the central aisle. "Otherwise we'll never get a pint."

A few others had beat them to the turnstiles, but the queue at the bar next door was still at a manageable level. Mark paid for two lagers and two packets of crisps, and with most seats already taken, carried them through to the garden.

"Cheers." Dave sat down and took a long drink. "That's better. Hey, I forgot to mention I saw you fighting with that bloke who came up to you in the pub."

"Not fighting as such." Mark winced. "He ducked."

"What's his problem?"

"He thinks I owe him money, but I don't."

"Oh, I see." Dave opened his packet of crisps. "Yeah, he's not the usual type you hang out with, for sure."

"I think he bats for the Middlesex Regiment."

"Absolutely." Dave nodded. "Even with *my* limited *gaydar* I can tell. You can, can't you?"

"Usually, yeah."

"For a moment I thought you'd turned."

"Bloody hell, no." Mark laughed and shook his head. "I put him right. He won't bother me again."

When the bar and garden became too crowded, it was time to go. As a passenger in Dave's van, Mark hid his surprise at the sight of Marie's car outside their flat.

"Thanks for the lift and the ticket, Dave. See you on Monday. Another week at the nursing home should do it."

"No probs. I'll be there from eight o'clock."

Mark let himself in the main door, and with some trepidation ran up the stairs to their flat.

CHAPTER TWELVE

"Glad you're back, baby." Mark held out his arms to Marie. "Let's start again, eh?"

"Have you had any more trouble from that bloke?" Marie walked towards him and put her arms around his waist. "Has he left you alone?"

"Yes." Mark kissed the top of Marie's head. "I haven't seen him for ages."

"I love you, Mark. Sorry I ran off like that."

"It doesn't matter. You're here now and we can get back to normal."

"Kiss me properly." She lifted her chin upwards. "None of this peck on the head bollocks."

Happy to oblige, Mark kissed Marie's lips and his tongue probed her open mouth. When he felt her fingers undoing the belt of his jeans, he pulled away.

"Steady on. I'm starving. Let's have some dinner first to give me some energy."

"Sounds interesting." Marie grinned. "An all-nighter?"

"Could be." Mark tried to keep his voice upbeat. "Depends who gives up first."

***

Mark lay wide awake in bed listening to Marie's soft snores. There was no real reason why their sex life should have suddenly taken a turn for the worse, especially with her new lacy baby doll nightie that would usually have failed to stay on for more than a couple of minutes. With a shameful and obvious failure to please her despite falling back on the same old pornographic videos locked away in his memory, he felt somehow less of a man. Hot and unable to settle, Mark eased himself out of bed, closed the bedroom door behind him, and clad only in a dressing gown padded out to the kitchen. He rubbed his eyes as the fluorescent light spluttered into life, then switched the kettle on.

"Come on, what the hell's going on here?" Marie yawned. "*Something* is, so don't lie and tell me *nothing* again."

Mark whirled around in surprise. Marie, suitably gowned, stood like a sentinel in the kitchen doorway.

"I thought you were asleep."

"I *was*, but as you know, it doesn't take much to wake me up. It's three o'clock in the morning, and I'm not going back to bed until you tell me what your problem is."

"I should think it's obvious, isn't it?" Mark took two cups off their hooks and added a tea bag to each. "You were there in the bed with me."

"If you're talking about *that*, then just forget it. I love you and it doesn't matter."

"It matters to *me*." Mark poured boiling water into the cups. "I've always been able to get an erection. I don't know why this is happening to me now."

"I'm sure it happens to all men at one time or another. It'll be fine. I'll get the milk, we'll have our tea, and then we'll go back to bed."

Back in bed with Marie's head on his shoulder and her right arm and leg across his body, Mark closed his eyes and waited for unconsciousness. When sleep eventually claimed him, Paul Mercer's face flitted in and out of various tormented dreams. He woke to the pleasant sensation of Marie stroking his erect penis.

"There." Marie sat up and straddled him. "I told you everything would be fine, didn't I?"

Deep inside her, he knew for certain that everything was *not* as it should be. Mark closed his eyes, conjured up the delicious sight of Paul lying naked on the same bed he now shared with Marie, and allowed himself to climax.

***

He parked his van in plain sight of the nursing home, then hopped out and walked around to the rear and undid the padlock on the back door. His bag of tools sat where he had placed them earlier that morning. Mark climbed into the van and rummaged around until he had found Paul's mobile number on the screwed up piece of paper he had carelessly thrown away. He sat on a reel of 1.5mm cable, committed the number to memory, but also stored it on his mobile just in case under the title *'Dave's New Phone'*. His face burned with the recollection of their lovemaking.

"Sorry I'm late." Dave knocked on the back of the van. "Blimey... you got a fever?"

"Just hot in these overalls." Mark shrugged. "Otherwise okay."

***

The Wybridge Arms was virtually empty at lunchtime. Mark scanned his surroundings with a practised eye, and simultaneously carried on a conversation with Dave and a few of the other subbies whilst trying not to appear too interested whenever somebody pushed open the main door. At the end of his working day he popped back to the pub for a swift half pint, but could only see a crowd of twentysomethings at the bar and two old men in one corner. He stared at Paul's number on his phone, then put the phone back in his pocket.

***

"You're home a bit later tonight." Marie appeared in the hallway and sniffed. "Have you been drinking?"

"I only had half of bitter with Dave to discuss some more work that might be available." Mark gave Marie a peck on the cheek. "I'd better let Rita know that I can work at the shop tonight. The contract at the nursing home is coming to an end, but the bills aren't."

"We're okay for now. You don't have to go to the shop. Stay here and we can have a cosy night in."

"I'd like to, but hey, the bills don't pay themselves."

Aware of her disappointment, Mark put his arms around Marie.

"I'll cook dinner tonight and wash up as well. You take it easy."

"It's a casserole. It's already in the oven."

"I'll stay home tomorrow night then." Mark took off his overalls and let them fall to the ground. "I'll bring home some steak or whatever you like."

"We can't afford steak. Get some fish and chips from that shop near the nursing home. That'll do me."

"Will do. We can cuddle up on the sofa... a kind of date night."

"I was hoping for more than that." Marie laughed. "You'll find out how much more tomorrow."

***

Bored beyond belief, his prayers were answered later that evening at the shop as he stacked baked beans in a pyramid style.

"The temptation to knock them all down is overwhelming." A hand placed one can of beans on top of the pile. "But hey, let *me* put the last one on."

"Paul." Mark's face flushed red. "What are you doing here?"

"The shop in Wybridge is closed. Two pints of milk and a loaf of bread please. Oh, and I'll take back that top can of beans if I may. Beans on toast for supper tonight."

"Be my guest." Mark stood back and indicated towards the pile with a wave of his hand. "Enjoy."

Mark made his way to the till, scanned in Paul's purchases, and tried unsuccessfully to stop the tremor in his hands.

"Have you got the DTs?" Paul laughed as he handed over some cash and then placed his goods in a bag. "You've got a bit of a shake there, mate."

"Been out on the piss last night."

"Must have been a good one."

"Yeah. Got totally bladdered."

"Well, good for you. See you around." Paul made his way to the door. "I'm off to enjoy my supper."

Mark held his breath in anticipation until Paul had closed the shop door behind him, then let out a sigh on hearing Rita's footsteps descending the stairs.

"You get off now, Mark, and I'll lock up. Do you want to work tomorrow evening?"

"Better not." Mark shook his head. "Marie's got something planned, I think."

"I'll wait to hear from you then."

Mark grabbed his jacket and hurried out the door, but Paul was nowhere to be seen. Dejected, he walked back to the flat where Marie briefly looked away from a TV programme to give him a smile.

"How'd it go?"

"Okay." Mark shrugged. "Rita wants me to work tomorrow."

"I thought we'd agreed to have a date night?"

"She needs me, I think. It's Thursday and there's always the weekend coming up."

"Well, make sure you tell her you've got something else to do on Saturday evening."

"Sure. Will do. I fancy some beans on toast. Want some?"

"No."

Mark, features creased into a grin, made his way to the kitchen, as a kind of delicious dread along with gnawing hunger burned like fire in the pit of his stomach.

CHAPTER THIRTEEN

The Wybridge Arms had been virtually empty again at lunchtime. Mark gathered up his tools and carried them down the stairs of the nursing home.

"All done?" Dave looked up from his clipboard as he signed out the last remaining subbies. "If you're free you can start that rewiring job I told you about the week after next."

"Yeah, I'm finished. Cheers for the heads-up… I'll start Monday week." Mark gave a brief nod to Dave. "I'll come back in a minute for the cables and ladders."

He looked left and right, but the street was quiet and empty of traffic. Mark stowed his tools in the back of the van, then returned to the nursing home and collected two reels of cable. On his way downstairs he saw Dave, cigarette in his mouth, standing outside on the front porch.

"How much longer are *you* here for, Dave?"

"About another week." Dave let out a cloud of cigarette smoke. "Some local artist has the job of painting a mural on the dining room wall, starting Monday… birds, bees, flowers… all that crap. Most of the time I'll leave him to it and head off to the pub, but I've still got to be around until he's done. He can always phone my mobile if there's a problem."

"What's his name?" Mark dug his fingers deeper into the cable.

"Paul something or other. He looked familiar. I'm sure I've seen him somewhere before."

"I've just remembered… I need to come back on Monday and run some routine tests on the control panel. Too late to do it now… Marie will do her nut if I'm not home for dinner on time tonight."

"Yeah, sure." Dave nodded. "Test away. There'll be nobody else here except us… oh …and that artist of course. I'll open up about half past eight."

"Great. See you Monday."

***

That evening the Mondeo seemed to make its own way to Sycamore Street. Mark parked the car a few yards down from number 92, then turned off the lights but remained in the driver's seat, feeling safe under the cover of darkness. Curtains still remained open in the front bay window, and he could see infrequent movements and the flicker of a TV screen. When a man walked past him up to the house and rang the doorbell, Mark slid down further in his seat.

Around ten o'clock when the curtains were closed, a full bladder necessitated a return to the flat. The expression on

Marie's face convinced him that any following conversation would not be particularly easy.

"I went to the shop tonight. I was lonely and just wanted to have a chat. Rita said you weren't working tonight, but you'd told me you *were*. So... where were you, Mark? Have you been seeing somebody else? It might explain why you're trying to avoid me all the time."

"Don't be silly." Mark's heart beat a tattoo in his chest. "Of course I'm not avoiding you. I *live* with you, don't I?"

"You're not answering my question. Where have you been all evening?"

"Out with Dave in the pub at Wybridge, if you must know. He gave me some more work for the week after next."

"If this happens again, I'm going to check with Dave. You've been acting weird lately, do you know that? *And...*I can't smell any beer like I usually can."

"I had a couple of vodka and tonics." Mark shrugged. "As far as I'm concerned I'm trying to earn enough money to put food on the table. Look... I've got one more day at the nursing home on Monday to run some tests on my fire alarm system, and then I've got the rest of next week off before I re-wire a four bedroomed house. If you can get one of those days off work we can go to the cinema or do something else you want to do."

"Promise?" Marie stood up from the settee and put her arms around his neck. "I hardly ever see you these days."

"Babe, we're no different from any other couple. We need to work to pay the bills."

"Sorry. I guess I'm overthinking again. I'll see if I can get Friday off and make it a long weekend. Perhaps we can go to the coast. But apart from that... have I got you all to myself this Saturday and Sunday?"

"Sure." Mark nodded, with more enthusiasm than he felt. "I'm all yours."

***

Senses on high alert, Mark signed his name on a timesheet that Dave had left in the Manager's office. Instead of immediately making his way to the fire alarm's control panel, he followed the sound of D.J Tiesto's 'Maximal Crazy' emanating from somewhere along the corridor. Mark opened the dining room door to find Paul at a table mixing paints on a palette.

"What the hell are *you* doing here?" Mark managed to feign just enough surprise to pass muster. "Are you stalking me?"

"The other way around, darling." Paul waved a paintbrush at him. "Gert saw you sitting outside my house in your car the other night."

"Must've been somebody else." Mark shook his head. "It wasn't *me*."

"Then it must have been your twin brother. As to what I'm doing here... I answered an advert for an artist to paint a mural for the old dears. I got the job. It'll take a week. More to the point... what are *you* still doing here? Dave said everything's finished now, apart from fitting the place out with furniture."

"I've still got a bit more work to do."

"Then I suggest you piss off and do it and leave me to paint."

Stung to the core, Mark turned on his heel and slammed the door.

"Alright, mate?" Dave appeared in the corridor. "I hate Trance, don't you?"

"Yeah." Mark nodded. "I told him to turn it down."

"Listen... I'm just popping out to put a bet on. There's nobody else due in until this afternoon, when the beds are arriving."

"No problem. It won't take me long to run the tests. I'll meet you in the pub at lunchtime if you like."

"Fine. Just sign the timesheet when you're done."

Mark made his way to the control panel at the foot of the stairs and set it to test. Within a few moments a wailing klaxon superseded D.J Tiesto at his finest hour.

"What the fuck's going on?" Paul, palette in hand, stomped along the corridor. "I can't hear myself paint!"

"How can you anyway, with that crap that passes for music you're listening to? I already told you... I have a bit more work to do which involves testing the fire alarm on this control panel here. No need to panic."

"I'm not panicking. I just want the fucking noise to stop."

"I'll stop it when I feel like it." Mark pressed another button on the control panel. "Fuck off, or I'll run one test after another."

"Not if I get hold of a hammer." Paul dropped the palette and looked around him. "I'll smash it to smithereens."

"Then I'll piss all over your mural."

Both panting and red-faced, Mark and Paul sized each other up like a pair of prize fighters. Paul moved closer to Mark and raised his right hand, knuckles white against his crimson shirt.

"I wouldn't advise that, darling." Mark's hands balled up into fists. "You might split your nails."

"You absolute arsehole." Paul hissed through clenched teeth. "I fucking love you though."

Time stood still. Mark felt as though his heart might burst open in that one exquisite moment. When Paul moved closer and kissed his lips, he offered no resistance.

"You took your bloody time, didn't you?" Paul held Mark at arm's length and grinned. "Jeez. I was hoping you'd knock at my door the other night."

"I didn't have the balls." Mark sighed. "I wanted to though. I've never done anything like this before. It's crazy."

"Hey, it's the UK, it's twenty twenty four, and being gay is not illegal anymore. We can even get married these days."

"I hope that's not a proposal. I think I'd need to marry a bird … if I ever do."

"Not after you've given *me* a chance. Anyway, leave me to finish this mural so I can get paid. Come round next Saturday morning and we can carry on where we left off."

"What about Gert?"

"He's just a friend. Actually his name is Roger."

"Roger?" Mark burst out into laughter. "He definitely looks more like a Gert."

"I'll tell him I'll be otherwise engaged." Paul ran one hand down the front of Mark's overalls. "He won't be watching *this* time. What will you do about your girlfriend?"

"I'll have to find the right words to tell her, but I'm not looking forward to it. All I've thought about since that night is *you*."

"I'll leave that job in your capable hands. Good luck. We can swap mobile numbers and keep in touch by text until Saturday."

When Paul kissed him again, Mark relaxed and felt as though he had arrived home in a safe harbour after days of being tossed about on a wild and stormy sea.

CHAPTER FOURTEEN

He needed enough whisky to give him courage, but not an excessive amount that could turn him into a blubbering fool. Mark glugged his third shot of spirit and stood up.

"Thanks for the drink, Dave. If you hear of any more work, just let me know."

"Will do. Don't forget to send your invoices in."

Mark strode out of the Wybridge Arms but avoided the nursing home, aware that Paul could still be working inside. He drove slowly to the flat, all the while mulling over the right words in his head which might cause Marie to be more sympathetic. Eventually the evil moment could be avoided no longer, and Mark turned his key in the front lock.

"Hi Babe, I'm home."

"You're done early today." Marie, hands covered in flour, came into the hallway. "That makes a nice change."

"Yeah, all done until next Monday."

"Rump steak tonight. They had a special on at the butcher's."

"Great." Mark moved towards Marie and put his arms around her. "Marie… dinner can wait a bit. I've got something to say. Wash your hands and come into the front room."

He flopped down upon the settee, hating himself for having to break up their world. When Marie hurried into the room and sat next to him, his heart rate immediately increased.

"Look... I love you, Marie..."

"But..."

"But... *yeah*...but...there's no easy way to say this."

"Say *what* exactly?" Marie stared at him. "That you've found somebody else?"

"I think so." Mark nodded. "But it's not another woman... he's a man."

"A *man*? You're *gay*?" Marie's mouth opened in surprise.

"Gay? Bi? Who knows?" Mark shrugged. "All I *do* know is that I love him, and he loves me. These last few weeks have been hell."

"Well, I knew *something* was up, but would never have guessed at *this*." Marie shook her head. "So what you're saying is that you'll be moving in with *him* and that *we're* finished. And so... by the way... no... I'm not going to be your Mary Austin."

"Who?" Mark felt a sob at the back of his throat. "Who are you talking about?"

"Freddy Mercury's girlfriend. She never left him, but let him alone to do his own thing. He gave her his house and his millions when he died though. I guess all I'll get from you is your drill, your ladders, and umpteen reels of cable."

"You can take what furniture you want, but don't make light of this. I'm so sorry." Mark wiped away tears. "I'm having enough trouble coming to terms with things myself, without *you* taking the piss."

"What else can I do? The whole scenario is farcical. Who is this guy? Do I know him?"

"He's the one that's been stalking me since I modelled at the art class."

"Don't tell me you're in love with the guy who kidnapped *me*?" Marie stood up. "What fucked-up kind of love is *that*?"

"I don't know, but I have to find out." Mark held out his arms. "Marie... can you ever forgive me?"

"No, I don't think so." Marie walked towards the door. "Get your own dinner. I'm packing and going back to my parents until I can find somewhere else to stay. D'you know what? You're the absolute worst person in the whole wide world. I hope you die of AIDS."

Mark sat rooted to the spot, sobbing, and unable to think straight when he stopped to consider how his life had changed in just a few short weeks. He finally admitted to himself he'd known he was somehow different from his classmates even way back when, but had buried the knowledge deep within and shut it away in a box.

When he heard the front door slam, he went to the window and looked down. Marie had opened a half can of magnolia paint he'd once used to decorate the kitchen with, and had poured it liberally over the roof of his Mondeo. Not wanting to cause a scene in the street and possibly neighbours getting the police involved, he allowed her to expunge her anger by slashing all four of his car's tyres with one of his own Stanley knives.

* * *

The week ahead stretched on forever. Mark kept himself busy with repairs to the Mondeo, worked long hours in the shop, and waited for his new life to begin. On the Friday evening his phone vibrated with a call, and Dave's number flashed up on the display screen.

"Hey Dave. How's it going?"

"They're moving the first of the oldies into the nursing home next week, but I don't know what they'll think about the mural."

"Why? What's wrong with it?" Mark tried to ignore a sudden sinking of his stomach.

"The whole of one wall is a garden, right? Flowers, trees, birds and bees and all that. He's done all that right."

"So?"

"Well… in the middle of the garden he's painted himself and another guy walking down a path holding hands. Er… the other guy looks a lot like *you*. In fact…yeah, it *is* you."

"Shit."

"Just thought I'd better let you know in case you get some funny looks in the pub at any time. The bloke must have a bit of a thing for you, I'd say."

"Thanks for the info, Dave." Mark felt glad Dave could not see the huge grin on his face. "Thanks very much."

THE END

THE BIRTHDAY PARTY

CHAPTER ONE

"Oh, my days!" Joy Metcalf shook the banner out of its plastic wrapper. "He really is as silly as arseholes."

"Who is?" Amber Richardson ceased arranging vol-au-vents and regarded her sister with interest through the kitchen's serving hatch. "What's up?"

"*Andrew*. Just look at what he's come back with." Joy, one hand on each end of the banner, raised her arms and opened it out above her head. "Only *he* would buy something like *this*."

"Dad won't even notice, and nor will any of the oldies." Amber's throaty laugh echoed around the empty hall. "I'll find a marker and stick a zero on."

"Well, hurry up then. They'll all be here in an hour or so."

Joy waved the banner at her brother as he walked into the hall carrying a stack of chairs.

"This is for a nine year old. Don't tell me... you picked all the others from the same pile as well."

"Dad won't give a monkey's." Andrew Perkins lowered the chairs down carefully. "You know he can't even read it unless he's got his glasses on."

"That's not the point, Andy. It just looks a bit slapdash."

"Yeah, well, that's me." Andrew turned towards the door. "I'll go and get some more chairs, seeing as nobody else is volunteering."

"I'll help you, Grandad." Mal Scott looked up from his iPhone. "I just need to send one more text."

"You'll have that etched on your epitaph." Andrew looked over his shoulder at his eldest grandson. "Here lies a bloke. He sent one more text and then he croaked."

"Very funny." Mal finished typing and stood up. "What needs doing?"

"You can put some tables along the back wall if you like." Amber carried a full tray of vol-au-vents from the kitchen. "Mum and I need to lay all the food out."

"Shall I put the cake on its stand now?" Denise Scott rubbed flour from her hands and walked into the community hall. "Auntie Amber, your hair looks nice, by the way."

"Thanks, I wondered if it was too dark."

"No, it's great. Makes you look younger."

Hey, at least Andy got *something* right... he bought two candles, a nine and a zero." Amber ran her fingers through dead straight locks. "The poor old boy would have needed his inhaler after trying to blow out ninety of them. Yeah, bring the cake out and put it on the centre table when Mal's done his bit."

Joy, banner over one shoulder, scraped a chair across the parquet floor towards Amber.

"Where's that pen? I'm going to stick this on the wall."

"Don't climb on the chair, *I'll* do it." Andrew took a biro from his top pocket. "That's all we need... *you* going base over apex."

"Okay, so I'm getting my state pension next year, but I'm not past it yet." Joy snatched the pen from Andrew and altered the banner. "You're not far behind me, little brother."

"Cheers for that." Andrew raised his right thumb. "I'll toddle off with my Zimmer frame in a while then and go and get the birthday boy."

"Don't worry, *I'll* do it in another half an hour. I expect Doris next door hasn't yet woke him up with her piano playing. Let's put some balloons up first. Did you get some?"

"Yeah." Andrew nodded. "They say *Get Well Soon.*"

"I wouldn't put it past you." Joy hissed through clenched teeth as she passed the banner to Andrew. "I should have bought them myself."

"Come on, give him a break, it's Dad's birthday." Amber laughed on her way back to the kitchen. "Let's play happy families."

A whoosh of wind; the door to the hall flew open, and a vision in pink leggings, a pink and white striped top and pink trainers barged through.

"I'm here now." Veronica Metcalf strode with purpose towards Joy. "Sorry I'm late, Mum. The cat was sick on my duvet."

"Lovely." Joy gave a fixed smile in Veronica's direction. "Fancy blowing up some balloons, Ronnie?"

"Is there a less energetic job? I've just put some more lipstick on."

"Perhaps help Amber and Denise in the kitchen then."

Joy watched her daughter's retreating back as Ronnie picked up speed again and waved at Amber through the hatch.

"Can I pinch a sarnie, Amber? I'm starving!"

To Joy's relief there were now enough willing helpers; the old boy hadn't yet offended the entire family. Joy passed Mal some balloons to inflate, and then accepted an incoming call.

"Hi, Cliff. Still not coming to the party?"

"You must be joking. I'm just the no-good son-in-law that never got a proper job, although probably I made more money self-employed than Billy ever did. I bet Lesley isn't there either."

"True." Joy agreed. "Probably she'll turn up sooner or later though, just to be with Andy."

"So what you're saying is that I should be there with *you*?"

"I'm not saying anything of the sort. At least if you're not here you won't be sitting in a corner of the hall and talking on your phone the whole time."

"*Someone's* got to bring the money in."

"So what *you're* saying is that I'm a lazy cow now I've retired?"

"Have a nice afternoon. Enjoy the party."

Joy, irritated, switched off her phone and threw it into her bag. Once again her husband had managed to get the last word in and end the call. To make matters worse, along the corridor in number 2, Doris had started to warm her fingers up.

CHAPTER TWO

The strains of 'Apple Blossom Time' jolted him awake. Billy Perkins glugged the rest of his apple juice, then threw a heavy book at the party wall as Doris Hennessey's reedy voice rose high above the thumping of piano keys. He shot the dagger of a stare right through the wall into what he imagined might be the piano's entrails. *What was the use of trying to make the old girl shut up when she never turned on her hearing aids?*

The doorbell chimed a cheap imitation of Big Ben's sonorous tones. With some difficulty Billy got to his feet, clung on to his walker, turned off the TV and shuffled to the front door.

"Who is it?"

"Joy."

It had always puzzled him why Elsie had insisted on naming their first daughter Joy. As a baby she had screamed night and day, and now the woman was as miserable as patients in a pox doctor's waiting room. Billy opened the door and stared at his daughter.

"What?"

"Hi Dad, I've come round to take you shopping."

"I don't need anything."

"Yes you do. You told me the other day you need some veggies. The mobile grocer's outside in his van. Come on, I'll help you choose."

He knew there would be no peace until his daughter had got her way. Billy settled his glasses more comfortably on his nose, fumbled for his wallet in his coat pocket, then pushed the walker out into the corridor and closed the front door behind him.

"We just have to go via the community hall for a minute. I've left my bag in there."

Billy knew it was futile trying to keep pace. He reached the hall a good two minutes behind Joy.

"Happy birthday!"

Joy smiled and beckoned him in. Billy, furious at being tricked, looked around him in horror. Ann, the warden, had an inane grin on her face, as did a few neighbours and several members of his family.

"I'm ninety, not nine." Billy pointed to a banner above the clock. "I don't want all this fuss."

"Stop being such a party pooper, Dad." Joy laughed and glanced at the banner. "Never mind, I must have forgotten to alter that one. There's lots of food. Beer too if you like. Denise threw out an olive branch and made you a cake. Come on, things are not *that* bad. Doris is coming along in a minute to play the piano. We can all have a sing-song."

"Fucking hell." Billy shook his head. "That's *all* I need."

"Don't swear. Be gracious, Grandad." Veronica ran forward and gave Billy a cuddle. "*I* had the cat throw up on my duvet. I nearly didn't make it here, but hey, here I am. Here *we* are, and now it's time to paartaay!"

"Where's Mavis?" Billy scanned the hall through rheumy eyes. "If I've got to be here, then I want Mavis here too."

"What number does she live at?" Mal stepped nearer to Billy. "I'll go and knock on her door."

"Number ten. *I'll* do it. She won't know who you are." Billy turned the walker around. "She might think you've broken in and are playing Knock Down Ginger."

"Playing *what*?" Mal's features took on a puzzled expression. "What's *Knock Down Ginger*?"

"Give me strength." Billy clattered out of the hall and down the corridor. "If it's not on their phones, the youngsters haven't got a clue."

He could hear Mavis's TV blaring out from the other side of the door. He clung to the walker with one hand, and pressed the bell several times with the other. Mavis, dressed in a totally unsuitable party frock, appeared before him.

"Yes, I'm coming to your party. Your daughter sent me an invite, but I wanted to watch the end of *Countdown* first." Mavis patted down a stray grey curl. "Shall we tell them, Billy? What do you think?"

"They'll have to know sooner or later, so yeah, let's do it." Billy nodded. "The shit's going to hit the fan though."

"We'll see it through together."

"Hurry up and get to the hall, Mavis." Billy lifted his walker to face the opposite direction. "All the neighbours are there, and Doris is going to bash the piano any minute now."

"God help us. I'll turn the television off and get my bag."

Billy moved at a snail's pace back along the corridor. By the time he arrived at the hall, Mavis had appeared by his side. Billy grabbed Mavis's hand and faced the crowd in front of them.

"I just want to say something."

Everybody around them grew silent. Billy could see Andy, Joy and Amber looking at him with less of their false bonhomie than usual. His legs ached and he wanted to sit down, but with Mavis's hand in his he felt that even at the grand old age of ninety he could still take on the world.

"Mavis and me... well... we're getting married."

Nobody spoke for at least 30 seconds until he heard Doris's execrable version of Mendelssohn's Wedding March start up. Ada at number four broke into spontaneous applause, followed by the rest of his neighbours. However, he noticed his daughters had remained silent as though rooted to the spot by shock.

"Well done, Dad!" Andrew laughed from the back of the room.

"Congratulations!" Ann ran towards Mavis and gave her a cuddle. "This is the first marriage we've had at the complex since I've been warden."

"Billy's the man for me." Mavis gushed. "I might need you to help me with all the arrangements though. No use asking *my* family."

"We didn't know anything about this." Joy looked at her siblings for confirmation. "Why didn't you tell us, Dad?"

"It only happened yesterday. There hasn't been time to tell *anyone*. Can I sit down now?" Billy's hands clutched his walker again as he moved forward. "I can't stand up for much longer."

"Give the birthday boy a seat!" Mavis trilled. "It's not every day you get married again at the age of ninety!"

Shepherded by Mavis, Billy flopped down into a high-backed armchair and sighed with relief.

"Thank Christ for that."

Out of the corner of his eye he could see Andrew approaching with a purposeful expression on his face, closely followed by both his daughters. He waved Mavis away, unwilling to let her hear what he knew would be forthcoming.

"Hey Dad." Andrew squatted down on his haunches. "You old bugger. What's going on?"

"Just what I told you." Billy shrugged. "I'm getting married."

"Does she know about your lottery win?" Joy, practical and down-to-earth as usual, handed Billy a can of lager. "Did you tell her?"

"No, I did not." Billy took a gulp of beer and shook his head. "Why should I? It's none of her business."

"She must have found out though." Amber smiled at her father. "Did you tell anyone else? You know what the grapevine's like around here."

"I don't remember if I did or not, but she hasn't mentioned it. Anyway, she'll know about it eventually when I buy a nice little bungalow somewhere and pay for some carers to make our last years together more comfortable."

"Dad... a bungalow will take quite a lot of your winnings, especially if you still want to live in Surrey."

"So? It's mine to spend as I like. Mavis likes the Isle of Wight anyway."

Billy finished the rest of his beer, and just for a split second enjoyed the look of disappointment on the faces of his offspring before they walked away.

CHAPTER THREE

Amber took a quick glance over her shoulder as she joined the queue for food behind Andrew. Mavis had already sidled back and sat herself down next to Billy, where they generally held court and chatted to party guests. She tapped her brother on the back.

"Andy, can I have a word outside in the garden?"

"Sure." Andrew nodded to Amber over his shoulder. "I just want to get a plateful before it all goes."

"Grab me a couple of sandwiches. I'll tell Joy to join us as well."

Amber left the queue and searched the room for her sister, whom she eventually found filling a large tea urn in the kitchen.

"Leave that. Come outside for a minute."

"Why?" Joy switched on the urn and took out several mugs from the cupboard underneath.

"I want to say something."

Amber hurried out of the hall then down the corridor and through the laundry room into the communal garden, where to her surprise she found Andrew already waiting.

"There's a quicker way through the fire door." Andrew handed a plate of food to Amber. "What's the big mystery?"

"Let's wait for Joy."

They ate in silence until the outer door to the laundry room flew open.

"What's going on?" Joy appeared with a plate of food in her hand.

Amber sighed.

"As you just heard, Dad's planning to buy a bungalow with Mavis using his lottery money. Once they get married Mavis will be his legal next of kin, and so you know what that means."

"We'll get fuck all." Andrew shrugged. "So what's new?"

"He's fifteen years older than her. She'll outlive him. She's got children, I *know* she has." Amber put her empty plate down on a nearby chair. "He hasn't even made a will. Unless he does, then Mavis's kids will inherit that bungalow."

"Like I just said… we'll get fuck all." Andrew popped a vol-au-vent into his mouth.

"Mum would have got Dad to see a solicitor had she still been alive. We'll have to do the same before he gets married." Joy snatched the last vol-au-vent from Andrew's plate.

"Hey, get your own!" Andrew swiped his plate higher in the air.

"She's a gold-digger. She *must* know about the win." Amber looked from Andrew to Joy. "We're his natural children. We're entitled to inherit."

"Not if he wants Mavis to have it." Andrew laughed. "Good luck with getting him to make a will. When has he ever agreed to do anything to suit anybody else but himself? I'm going back in… they'll wonder what we're doing out here."

"Andy… wait a minute." Amber hurried after her brother. "She'll get him to herself if they move to the Isle of Wight. We can't keep paying out for ferry crossings."

"So let them get on with it. Accept that you'll never get your hands on upwards of a million quid."

"What do you think, Joy?" Amber stopped at the door. "Shall we try and get Dad to make a will?"

"We can try, but right now Andy's right… we need to get back to the party."

The strains of 'Roll Out the Barrel' echoed down the corridor as Amber, followed closely by Joy, slipped into the hall as unobtrusively as possible. Amber bridled at the sight of Mavis stroking her father's arm. Mavis' eyes held a glint of unadulterated triumph.

"Joy, that woman's gloating." Amber hissed over her shoulder. "We've got to do something about her."

"After *you* with the arsenic, darling." Joy whispered whilst smiling at a row of elderly people seated around the periphery of the hall. "But don't do it just yet."

Neighbours who could stand for a longer amount of time had gathered around the piano. Amber put her hands on Doris's shoulders and bent over to shout in her ear.

"Can you play *A Nightingale Sang in Berkeley Square*? It's Dad's favourite song."

"I can play anything." Doris shouted. "As long as it's in the key of C."

Out of the corner of her eye, Amber saw her father slowly struggle to his feet and move towards the piano as Doris struck the first few notes. The song had obviously brought back memories of long ago when they had been a tight unit of five. Amber stood up straighter and clutched Billy's thin upper arm.

"Doris is playing your song, Dad." Amber looked at Mavis over the top of Billy's head. "Dad used to sing this song to my mother when we were kids."

She was pleased to see how Mavis's genial expression had faltered for just an instant. Amber put one arm around her father's shoulders and sang with him the words he had taught her in childhood.

"Get Doris a drink." Billy wiped a tear from his eye. "She deserves one."

"Now you'll be able to sing it to *me*." Mavis moved in on the other side of Billy and gave him her handkerchief. "I don't know this song very well, but I'm willing to learn."

Triumph had returned to Mavis's features. Doris brought the tune to a pounding finish. Amber stomped towards the temporary bar set up at the kitchen hatch. She needed a drink much more than Doris did.

CHAPTER FOUR

Mal, bored witless, played another game of Angry Birds on his iPhone and then looked around the hall. Apart from his sister and aunts, there wasn't a female there less than three hundred years of age. He focused on his great-grandfather and Mavis, who had a proprietary air as she fussed around the old boy. He came to the sad conclusion that even his ninety year old great-grandfather received more female attention than he, Mal, would probably ever get. He tried to imagine the two of them having sex, but decided the possibility was just too outrageous to contemplate.

He skimmed through a couple of messages from his best mate Lewis. The sound of the piano grated on his nerves, and he had no idea what they were all singing about. His two great-aunts stood whispering in a corner. Mal decided to fill his plate for a second time. He stood up and made his way to the buffet, to find his mother and grandfather already there.

"Alright, boy?"

"Not really, Grandad." Mal took the last three ham sandwiches. "Nobody talks to me, and the music sucks."

"Do your best and endure it for another couple of hours."

"Take no notice of him, Dad." Denise waved an arm in Mal's direction. "It's what's known as the Generation Gap."

Marl pulled a face at his mother, and added two chocolate éclairs to his stash of food.

"Malcolm, don't take any more." Denise shook her head. "There'll be nothing left otherwise."

"When can we go home?" Mal took a large bite of an éclair and briefly checked his phone again. "I'm bored."

"Go and ask Aunt Joy or Aunt Amber if there's anything you can do."

"Have I got to, Mum?" Mal checked his display screen to find a joke from Lewis. "All they do is whisper to each other. What's going on with those two?"

"Whatever it is, it's none of your business." Denise waved Mal away with one hand. "Go and be sociable, and for God's sake put that bloody phone away."

Mal finished his plate of food then sidled nonchalantly to where his two great-aunts still stood in heated conversation. Gazing at his phone's screen, he sent a joke back to his friend but all the while kept his ears attuned to his aunts' voices. He heard the mention of a million pounds and a tin box under the bed, and moved in closer. His phone pinged with a picture of a naked woman, but Mal was too intent on his mission to reply to Lewis. He made a *tut* of annoyance as the old girl they called Doris started up again with another song, which now made it virtually impossible for him to hear what was going on.

"Alright, Mal?" Amber smiled with sudden false joviality. "Enjoying yourself?"

"Yeah, ta." Mal nodded and held up his phone. "Sorry, just got a call from a mate. I've got to phone him back."

Several partygoers now sang 'Maybe It's Because I'm a Londoner' rather too loudly for Mal's liking. He made his way through the throng around Doris, and then out into the corridor and through the laundry room to the communal garden, letting his eyes drift once more to his display screen to savour the naked girl. His penis danced a jig in his trousers. He sent a message to Lewis to tell him to stop sending pictures of naked girls at his great-grandad's birthday party. He surreptitiously adjusted his trousers just as his grandfather appeared in the garden clutching a pint of beer.

"Okay?"

"Yeah, Grandad. Do you know what?"

"No, what?" Andrew took a large gulp of beer.

"Aunt Amber and Aunt Joy were talking about a million pounds. I just heard them."

"Did you indeed?" Andrew regarded Mal with a quizzical expression. "That'll be about Dad's lottery win I expect."

"Did he win the lottery then?" Mal slid his phone into his pocket. "Mum never said."

"Yes he did, last year. Almost a million pounds, you heard right."

"Cool!" Mal, naked photos forgotten, stared at his grandfather.

"But don't expect any of it. He's as tight as a crab's arse, and that's watertight. You might as well whistle Dixie." Andrew finished the last dregs of beer. "He's more likely to give it to the dogs' home than us, especially after your father pissed him off."

Mal, a wave of disappointment washing over him, grabbed his phone again as he felt it vibrate. His WhatsApp icon showed a red '1'. He tapped the green square to be confronted by a girl who possessed the biggest bazoomas he had ever seen, just as his grandfather deposited his empty glass on a bench and turned towards the complex.

"Come back inside, Mal."

"Yeah, I've just got to send a text."

"Ye Gods."

Mal waited until the garden was empty before searching his contacts for Lewis's number.

"Listen, you wanker, I'm at a family do. It's my great-grandad's ninetieth party. Don't send any more just yet."

"She was hot, wasn't she?" Lewis giggled. "Just what the birthday boy needs."

"It'll kill him." Mal laughed along with Lewis. "Hey, I've just found out he won the lottery last year."

"Yeah? How much?"

"Nearly a million quid. Imagine that!"

"Ninety years old with a million quid?" Lewis' voice rose a couple of semitones. "You've got to get some of that, mate."

"No chance. He hates my dad, and he doesn't speak to my mum much because she married Dad against his wishes."

"Dave? He's great." Lewis cleared his throat. "Especially after he mended my bike when the shop wanted eighty quid."

"They just rub each other up the wrong way. Gotta go now."

"Piss off then."

Mal laughed, ended the call, and made his way towards the door to the laundry room.

CHAPTER FIVE

Mavis Renshaw sat as close as she could to Billy, and enjoyed her new-found status of being affianced after 25 long years of widowhood. In order to have had a better life, Billy was the man she should have married in the first place, but of course he had spent the best years of his life married to somebody else, producing three children that should have been hers. Instead she had given birth to two wastrel sons who had obviously taken after their toe rag of a father.

She saw the neighbours' surreptitious glances in her direction, but today was hers and Billy's day, and a time for celebration. Mavis was the cat with the cream, whatever the crotchety, jealous old women thought. She also sensed that Billy's children were not keen on the fact their father had decided to marry again, especially the youngest one. Mavis preferred the son to the two daughters; at least he had offered half-hearted congratulations. Still, she would smile, nod, appear gracious, and refuse to let the daughters' daggers of hatred pierce her heart.

"Enjoying yourself, Billy?" Mavis leaned into Billy's good ear. "What's it like being ninety?"

"Fucking awful. I can't wait to get back to my flat."

"Now now." Mavis giggled. "You're loving all the attention really. Billy…I've got one question for you."

"What?"

"When am I going to get an engagement ring?"

"Look at the state of me, Mavis. How the hell am I supposed to get out to the shops to buy one?"

"I've still got my car. We can go together and choose one if you like."

"Tell you what." Billy took a sandwich from a tray held by Veronica and then turned towards Mavis. "*I'll* give you the money, and *you* go out and buy one. I can't walk too far these days."

"You'll still need to go to the bank."

"No. I've got some money in my flat." Billy chewed the sandwich. "I'll give you five hundred. That should do it."

"You're very generous, Billy."

"It's my middle name."

"You shouldn't keep all that money in your flat."

"Why? Are you going to pinch it, then?"

"No, of course not." Mavis looked at Billy, surprised. "Whatever made you think that?"

A tap on her shoulder caused Mavis to turn around. There, more smartly dressed than she had ever seen him before and reeking of cheap after shave, stood her youngest son.

"Peter!" Mavis, embarrassed, stood up and kissed the idler who had never had a job in his entire life. "How nice that you're here! I didn't see you come in. When I told you about the party I didn't expect you to turn up."

"I crept in. When I found out you were getting married, I wanted to meet my new step-dad-to-be." Peter Renshaw focused on Billy as he bent over to hug his mother. "Can I call you *Dad* yet?"

"No you can't." Billy shook his head. "I'm not your father, so *Billy* will do."

"Righto."

Mavis, eager to bridge a sudden chasm of silence, blurted out the first thing that came into her head.

"Billy's going to give me some money to buy an engagement ring."

"Well, that's fantastic." Peter glanced at the bare ring finger on his mother's left hand. "I'll come with you and help you choose it."

Mavis watched with some concern as Peter made his way over to the buffet, piled food high onto a paper plate, and then stuffed a whole sausage roll into his mouth while helping himself to another three.

"He looks as though he hasn't eaten for a week." Billy curled his upper lip. "In a minute, between him and Mal, there won't be anything left for the rest of us."

Billy was not the only person in the room besides herself who had noticed her son's gluttony. The resulting body language detected in a short, sharp conversation between Joy and Peter convinced Mavis that Peter would not be taking any more food. She turned her attention to Denise, who was tapping on the side of a glass with a spoon.

"Attention all! I hope you're all having a good time. In about half an hour we'll sing to the birthday boy and cut the cake, so get your vocal cords lubricated with lots of tea."

"I'd rather have another beer." Billy mumbled between mouthfuls of prawn vol-au-vent. "Denise's tea is always piss-poor."

"I heard that, Grandad. No cake for you." Denise wafted by on a cloud of perfume.

"You've probably put arsenic in it anyway." Billy winked at Denise. "It's not really piss-poor, I'm just a grumpy old man."

Mavis acknowledged Peter, who held his plate aloft then sat down beside her on the floor just as he had done over 50 years ago before his separation anxiety had fled forever.

"Any news of your brother?"

"I haven't heard anything from him, Mum." Peter took a bite of a ham sandwich. "Last I heard he was being dried out in the QEQM Hospital."

"He still lives in Margate?"

"He *did*, I don't know if he does now. When shall we go shopping for your ring? Tomorrow?"

"Why do you want to come with me? I wouldn't think it's your thing."

"I haven't seen you for ages. Can't I spend some quality time with my mummy?"

Mavis tried to remember the last occasion she had spent quality time with either of her sons. She settled for twenty five years previously at their father's funeral while they waited for the will to be read.

CHAPTER SIX

Peter Renshaw took a sideways glance at the decrepit old man who would soon become his stepfather, and found to his surprise that the old boy was already sizing *him* up. He could hardly believe how excited his mother had been to impart her news in one of their rare phone calls, but *who in their right mind would marry somebody aged ninety?* The old boy would obviously not live much longer, and therefore must have more money than his mother had previously thought; there could be no other reason for her sudden dash to the altar after a quarter of a century of living contentedly alone.

Under Billy's scrutiny, Peter felt anger slowly bubbling to the surface. Unwilling to make a scene, he moved away from his mother and scanned the room. He was one of the youngest by far, apart from a miserable-looking teenager checking his phone in one corner. A clatter of walking sticks falling to the floor interspersed the constant chatter of elderly residents all grateful for somebody to talk at. His mother's voice rose higher and higher as she held court over the general hubbub. The teenager looked the safest option.

Peter ambled towards Mal who, unaware of anybody's presence, scrolled through countless virtual pages.

"Anything worth looking at?" Peter settled himself next to Mal and peeped over the boy's shoulder.

"No." With one flick of his wrist Mal pocketed his phone. "What's it to you, anyway?"

"Lighten up. I've looked at more porn than you've shaken your dick at."

Relieved to see the boy's mouth turn up at the corners, Peter settled back further in his chair.

"I'm Peter. Who the fuck are *you*? Not much of a rave up is it?"

"It's my great-grandad who's ninety. I'm Malcom...well...*Mal* really. I had to come along to help set it all up. I haven't seen *you* before either."

"I'm Mavis's son – you know... the son of the woman who's marrying Billy."

"Yeah, Mavis." Mal hacked a glob of phlegm from the back of his throat. "My great-aunts reckon your mum is after his lottery winnings."

"Yeah, I heard he won the lottery." Peter could have bitten out his tongue as sat up straighter in his chair. "How much?"

"Nearly a million quid I heard them say. How did *you* find out?"

"Well, word gets about, doesn't it? Anyway…colour me *happy*. My mum had better get him to the altar quick then, what d'you think?"

Peter looked across the room at his mother, who chatted to neighbours whilst fussing over Billy at the same time. Knowing how she had always been ready to share anybody's secret in idle gossip, Peter could only guess at the difficulty she must be having at keeping the knowledge of Billy's win to herself.

"And it's probably under his bed."

"*All* of it?" Peter, mouth open with incredulity, turned to Mal.

"Don't know." Mal shrugged. "All I *do* know is that he can't get to the bank much anymore, and I've often wondered why he always keeps his bedroom door locked when he's not in there. I've never been allowed in the bedroom."

"Good idea to keep it locked." Peter's mind raced with a thousand thoughts. "You never know who's hanging about these places, do you?"

"How did *you* get in? Do you know the code on the main door?"

"I followed behind one of the oldies as they got out of their car and punched in the code. I said I was going to see Mavis, my mum, and they told me she was in the hall."

"They're not supposed to let anybody in."

"Well, I'm hardly *anybody*, am I? I'm Mavis's son." Peter gave a 'tut' of annoyance. "Jeez, anyone would think I'm Jack the frigging Ripper."

"So why aren't you sitting with your mum, then?"

Peter had heard enough, and had tired of the irritating teenager. He stood up.

"Nice meeting you. Go back to your porn until they cut the cake."

The boy had already whipped the phone out of his pocket. Peter grabbed a can of lager from the buffet table and wondered how the hell he could find out which flat was the old man's without anybody looking at him with overt suspicion. It was time to sidle out into the corridor to see if he could nab a late arrival before they shuffled into the hall.

Away from the noise of the party, the corridor leading to all ten flats was completely empty. Peter checked the ceiling for cameras, but could see none. He started at the first flat and pulled a handle to a box-like structure sitting about shoulder height to the left of the front door. To his surprise the front of the box folded down halfway to reveal several letters and another small opening on the opposite inner wall allowing the post to be accessed from inside the flat. He pushed one hand in and checked the name and address on an envelope before closing the mailbox again and moving on. All flats had similar mailboxes to the first one. At flat number 5 he found a letter addressed to a Mr William Perkins. Peter grinned, replaced the letter where he had found it, and checked the front door. Locked, as he would have expected. He hurried back to the community hall and as far as he could tell, nobody had even noticed his absence.

The old boy had fallen asleep in his chair; the excitement of the party obviously too much for him. More importantly was a bunch of keys dangling precariously from one gnarled fist. Peter made his way towards where his mother still sat next to Billy and chatted incessantly to a neighbour on the opposite side.

"How's it going, Mum?" Peter bent over his mother and kissed her forehead, while whipping Billy's keys from his hand at the same time and pocketing them in an instant. "Lovely party."

"Yes, it is, but they'll let Billy sleep for a while before they do the cake I expect." Mavis looked up and smiled. "Perhaps pass around some food. It's all got to be eaten."

"Sure." Peter stood up straighter. "Will do."

He would carry out his mother's request, and then it was time to strike while the iron was still hot. His mother would be proud of him. Apart from the party, Peter doubted whether Billy ever ventured out of his flat. It was now or never.

***

Nobody had made any effort to talk to him all the while he handed out plates of sandwiches. Peter waited until Doris had resumed playing after a sherry break, checked the corridor was still clear, and then made his way to Flat 5. There were 3 keys on the ring and one other smaller key, and the third one he tried fitted easily into the front door lock.

There was an aroma of either broccoli or cabbage. Peter wrinkled his nose, pulled his shirt sleeve down over his right hand, and closed the front door behind him. The first key opened an inner door off a small corridor and Peter took a quick glance around Billy's sparsely furnished bedroom, which consisted of a single bed with what he surmised was a red night alarm pull cord above it, a wicker chair, a small wardrobe, and a chest of drawers. Keeping his fingers covered by his shirt sleeve, Peter riffled through Billy's underwear in the chest of drawers, then checked pockets of the old boy's jackets and trousers in the wardrobe. Undeterred, he stood on the chair and checked on top of the wardrobe, then got down on his knees and looked under the bed. Within kicking distance close to the edge of the bed he could see a padlocked wooden box. The smaller key on the ring opened the box to reveal what Peter surmised to be around forty thousand pounds.

"Fuck me slowly!"

Peter stood up and made his way to the kitchen, where four supermarket carrier bags lay folded on a shelf. The third key he had not yet used fitted into the door leading to a communal garden where from behind Billy's net curtains he could see a few party guests had convened. Taking one of the bags he went back into the bedroom, scooped all the notes from the box into the bag, then locked the box and kicked it back under the bed. With the bag in one hand he locked the bedroom, then checked the outer corridor once more before securing the front door. Propping the main entrance door open with a fire extinguisher, he ran to his beat-up Ford Fiesta, threw the supermarket bag into the boot, put the fire extinguisher back in its place, then hurried back in to join the party.

CHAPTER SEVEN

Mabel's strident tones pushed through his dreams.

"Wake up, Billy. It's time to light the candles on the cake. Everyone's waiting to serenade you."

Billy felt tired. Used to his normally quiet existence, the sound of people singing and laughing, Doris's piano playing, and his family's constant attention had caused a weariness he had not experienced since a mild dose of Covid during Lockdown. Embarrassed to have fallen asleep at his own party, Billy struggled to banish the fog swirling around in his head.

"You dropped these on the floor."

Billy knew one thing as clear as day... he did not like or trust Mabel's son. He grabbed the keys from Peter and put them in his trouser pocket. The keys felt hot, as though they had been in the bastard's hands for hours.

"I didn't drop them."

"Don't be churlish." Mabel turned her head towards Billy. "Peter's done you a favour. You fell asleep and dropped your keys. He found them and picked them up for you. Come on, up you get. Let's go over to the cake."

With considerable effort, Billy rose to his feet and clenched both fists around the handles of his walker. Just like Moses as he parted the Red Sea, several people stood back to give Billy unfettered access to the buffet table.

"I'm going to light the candles, Grandad, and then we'll all sing." Denise struck a match. "Is everyone ready?"

"Please don't." Billy shook his head. "Not on my account."

"Take your punishment like a man." Andrew laughed. "It's not every day you get to be ninety."

"I don't want to be ninety, I'd rather kick the bucket. Old age is no fun." Billy's legs felt leaden. "Get this thing over with and then I can go and sit down."

With a forced smile Denise lit the two blue candles on top of the cake. Doris struck up 'Happy Birthday', and all partygoers erupted into song. Billy, a pained expression on his face, waited until the room had quietened down to blow both candles out.

"Congratulations!" Joy kissed Billy on one cheek. "Did you make a wish?"

"Yeah. I wished this fucking party would come to an end."

"Don't be so miserable." Mavis patted Billy's hand. "Go back to your chair and I'll bring you a piece of cake."

Billy turned the walker around and shuffled to his seat. Veronica held out a glass of Guinness in his direction.

"There you go, Grandad. It'll put hairs on your chest."

"That's better." Billy took a slurp of the dark liquid. "Things are looking up at last. Are you still living with that idiot?"

"No." Veronica threw her head back and laughed. "Somebody else has him now. Why are you getting married, Grandad? Nobody gets married these days."

"I want to make an honest woman of Mavis. I don't like all this living in sin business."

"But you're not living in sin. Mavis has her flat and you have yours."

"It's what people of my generation do when they fall in love."

"Have it your way, Grandad." Veronica kissed Billy on the forehead. "Can I be a bridesmaid then?"

"We'll probably just have a quiet wedding in the Grange Hotel. No need for bridesmaids. We had all that when I married your grandmother."

Billy looked up as Mavis approached holding a piece of birthday cake wrapped in a serviette. She handed the cake to Billy then looked at Veronica with interest.

"Mavis, this is Veronica, my granddaughter. She wants to be our bridesmaid."

"You're a bit old for that, aren't you?" Mavis seated herself beside Billy again. "It's not going to be a big wedding."

"Hmm … I *could* say the same to you." Veronica gave Mavis an icy stare. "My grandad's ninety for God's sake and *you're* not far off… why bother getting married at all?"

"I'm seventy five actually." Mavis's voice rose a few semitones. "And I'll thank you to mind your own business."

"I'm forty two… young enough not to need retirement living, inco pads and Velcro shoes."

"I still wear stilettos." Mavis sniffed.

"Ladies… ladies… enough." Billy downed the rest of his Guinness. "Who's going to get me another Guinness?"

"*I* will, Grandad." Veronica laughed out loud. "But don't have any more, or you'll start trying to crawl into your Velcro shoe."

Billy watched his granddaughter's retreating back, then turned to Mavis.

"She's a bit highly strung, that one. Just put up with them all until the party's over. None of them will come around again until I'm dead."

"I'm sure that's not true, Billy. You must have had your family visiting you at one time or another."

"Only when they wanted something."

"What did they want?"

"Huh!" Billy rubbed his right thumb against his forefinger. "Money. What else?"

CHAPTER EIGHT

Veronica Metcalf poured some of the contents from a can of Guinness into a half pint glass.

"Mum, the last thing Grandad needs is to get shit-faced at his own party."

"He'll notice it's only half a pint." Joy took some more sausage rolls out of the oven. "He's not that daft."

"I don't like Mavis. She's rude. Apparently I'm too old to be a bridesmaid."

"You won't be a bridesmaid because that wedding will not go ahead. I've heard she's got two dodgy sons, and one of them has been creeping around here all afternoon. They're after his money, I know it. I'm going to have serious words with your grandfather in the very near future."

"If he's in love then he's not going to listen, is he? Would *you* have listened if Grandad had told you not to marry Dad?"

"He *did* tell me, most emphatically." Joy laughed. "And yes, I took not a bit of notice. I haven't regretted it though. But

I knew Dad wasn't after my money, because at the time I didn't have any."

"Why on earth does he need to get married at *his* age?" Veronica shrugged her shoulders. "Let's face it, he's probably only got a few more years left."

"No doubt she's pressured him into it. He's her meal ticket for the next twenty five years."

Veronica popped a hot sausage roll into her mouth and made her way back into the hall, noticing how her grandfather's eyes followed the glass of Guinness in her hand.

"I wanted a pint, not a half."

"Sorry, Grandad, there aren't any more pint glasses."

"Then get me another one of *these*."

"*I'll* get it for him." Mavis stood up. "You sit and chat with your grandfather for a minute."

Veronica waited until Mavis had disappeared into the kitchen, and then plumped herself down in the woman's still-warm seat.

"Grandad..."

"What?" Billy took a long swig of Guinness.

"*Who* asked *whom* for their hand in marriage?"

"We talked about it in bed yesterday morning." Billy cackled. "We both agreed it was a good idea."

"She gets in your bed?" Veronica took a deep breath of surprise.

"No. I get in hers. I've only got a single bed, but she's got a double."

"Be careful, Grandad."

"Why? She's hardly going to get pregnant, is she?"

"I didn't mean *that*..."Veronica moved a hand in front of her mouth momentarily to stifle a giggle. "I meant... you know... your lottery win."

"You're the second person who's mentioned that today."

"Grandad, it *has* to be mentioned, because if you marry Mavis then she will end up with it."

"And so she should, as my wife." Billy sighed with irritation. "Did *you* want the money then?"

"No, of course not. I'll be carrying on with Dad's business when he retires."

"Selling sex toys and ladies' underwear?"

"There's a lot of money in it."

"I won't be buying any."

"Lots of other people will. Anyway, Mavis has another drink for you." Veronica stood up. "I'll let her have her seat back."

Veronica gave a half-smile to Mavis then made her way to the piano, where Joy stood with a group of elderly people all singing '*Call Round Any Old Time*'. She hissed in her mother's ear.

"Mum."

"What?"

"They're having sex."

"Who are?" Joy stopped singing and looked around the hall in alarm.

"Grandad and Mavis. He told me he gets in her bed. I bet she seduced him in her baby doll nightie."

"Good God, I don't want to think about it. However did you bring *that* subject up?"

"I didn't. I asked who popped the question to whom, and he said they *both* talked about it in bed yesterday morning."

"Oh, my word."

"I had to try really hard not to laugh. I mean... he's ninety and she's no spring chicken."

"This is getting worse." Joy ran one hand through her hair. "She's lured him in with sex. I suppose he hasn't had any for years. Even Mavis must look like Raquel Welch in his situation."

"Who?"

"Just leave me to think about this a bit more, Ronnie. I need to speak to the others."

CHAPTER NINE

Billy had had enough. The Guinness had begun to take effect, and he felt overwhelmingly weary. He stood up and swayed slightly, clutched his walker, and waited for the latest singalong to cease before shouting out loud to nobody in particular.

"It's been a lovely party, and thanks to my family who arranged it. I'm tired now and I'm going back to my flat. For those who arrived by car, I hope you all have a good journey home."

To his annoyance Doris started straight away on the next song as though she had not heard a thing he'd said; now he would be forced to listen to his own party in his bedroom when he tried to have a rest.

Irritated beyond measure, Billy said his goodbyes to Mavis and his children, and made for the exit whilst attempting to dodge well-wishers. Relieved, he unlocked his front door, stepped over the threshold, and then unlocked the bedroom. A whiff of perfume hit his nostrils at once. Billy, puzzled, eventually came to the conclusion the warden must have slipped in to do her monthly check of the night alarm whilst he'd been at the party. As far as he was concerned, the stench reminded him of yellow urinal blocks the warden placed in the visiting men's lavatory. He opened the window, sat carefully on the side of his bed, then laid himself down and put his head on the pillows.

When an insistent knocking pierced his dreams, it seemed as though he had only just nodded off to sleep. Billy yawned, got up off the bed, and with the aid of his walker made his way to the front door to be confronted by Mavis.

"It was a bit rude of you to leave the party. I came by to see if you're all right."

"Of course I'm all right." Billy shrugged. "Why wouldn't I be? I was just tired."

"Well, they've all gone now. Are you sure you don't want to come with me tomorrow to choose an engagement ring?"

"No, I'll leave that to you. Come in and wait in the front room, and I'll get you some money for it."

With Mavis safely installed in his best armchair, Billy grabbed his keys from the hook then trundled back into the bedroom. With his left foot he felt under his bed for the money box, which did not seem to be in the same position as it was before. He kicked it towards his walker, then bent over and picked it up. It felt much lighter than it usually did. With trembling fingers he rested the box on his chest of drawers and unlocked it, then with a stab of shock stared at the empty interior in horror.

"Call the police! I've been robbed!"

"What?" Mavis appeared in the doorway. "Did you say you've been robbed?"

"Yes! Look!" Billy showed Mavis the empty box. "Somebody's stolen all my money!"

"You haven't put it somewhere else, have you?" Mavis's eyes searched the room. "Who knew you kept it here?"

"No-one. I keep the bedroom door locked at all times."

"Well, nobody else has the keys, do they? I can see the window hasn't been tampered with. I'll go and find Ann." Mavis turned on her heel and made for the door. "Let's see if she knows anything about it."

Billy, dejected, looked once more in vain at the empty box as though willing the notes to reappear, and then sat on the edge of his bed with the box under his arm. Mavis reappeared with the warden in tow.

"I've called the police, Billy." Ann strode into the bedroom. "How much money have you lost?"

"A lot." Billy sighed and sniffed. "Let's just say… a lot. Some bastard has been in here and stolen it."

"I'm the only one with a master key, but you know *I* haven't taken it. I didn't even realise you had any money in here." Ann sat down beside Billy. "We'll get to the bottom of this. Don't worry."

"*Her* son's had it. I know." Billy pointed a finger at Mavis. "He handed me my keys at the party."

"You can't blame Peter." Mavis shook her head. "You'd fallen asleep and dropped them on the floor. He picked them up for you. He's been at the party all the time. He's only just left."

"No he wasn't. I'm going to tell the police."

"You can't accuse my son without good solid evidence. I'm going back to my flat now. This is madness. Forget about an engagement ring… I refuse to speak to you again unless you come to your senses and stop picking on my son."

Before he could utter a reply, Mavis marched out of the bedroom and slammed Billy's front door hard behind her.

"I *am* right, you know." Billy turned to Ann. "That chap's no good. He even *looks* shifty."

"Tell the police about your thoughts when they get here. Leave it to them to find out who did it." Ann stood up. "Right now I'll go and tell your family and help them clear up. Your children will be along to see you in a minute, I'm sure."

CHAPTER TEN

Peter Renshaw could hardly believe his good fortune as he strolled leisurely around the Ford showroom. He had counted the money three times in the privacy of his flat, and knew he could afford the brand new black Kuga he'd had his eyes on for the past half an hour and still have a few hundred quid left over. However, the thought of handing over £37,999.99p in cash was a little daunting. Should he wait until any police investigations had been carried out? The old man would undoubtedly have already phoned them and relayed his suspicions. It would be unwise to pay the whole sum into his bank, which had only ever known benefit payments, and he could hardly ask his mother to watch it. He did not know of anybody else who might want to keep hold of it for him; the only other thing he could think of was to bury the money for the time being.

"Can I help you, Sir?"

A particularly unctuous salesman had been following him around surreptitiously for ages. Peter shook his head.

"Just looking, thanks."

Disappointed, the salesman slunk back to his desk. Peter, deep in thought, walked away, an idea forming in his head. Maybe if his brother still lived in the tower block opposite Margate Seafront next to The Promenade restaurant and was still on the sauce, then a little bit of bribery with a brandy bottle or two might just do the trick. His heap of a car would never make the long journey and he'd need to get rid of it, but just around the corner from Phil's flat was Margate train station. He would buy a single ticket and aim to lie low at the seaside for a few months.

Back home, a couple of deadbeats waited for the lift as Peter opened the downstairs community door. The lift doors opened and a stench of urine permeated the foyer. Peter wrinkled his nose and avoided eye contact with the two youths until the lift reached the eighth floor.

"This is my floor." Peter pushed past and hurried out of the lift. "Ta."

The council had boarded up yet another flat on the eighth floor landing. Peter unlocked his front door, flicked the light switch, and grimaced as once again discovered the electric meter needed feeding. He had enough cash to run the thing for years now, but decided to stay frugal and give the council just enough money for an overnight stay.

***

A stiff breeze hit him in the face as Peter, bag of cash in hand, strolled out of Margate station and turned right past The Promenade restaurant. Phil's tower block now stood directly in front of him, faded, jaded, and down-at-heel. A sheet-like banner hung from one of the top floor windows boasting the mis-spelt slogan 'Support Greenpeas'. Peter laughed and made his way to the entrance to find the key code vandalised, the main door hanging off its hinges, and all glass windows in the foyer smashed. A lop-sided notice on the lift door read 'Out of Order'.

Peter gave a 'tut' of annoyance, then took the stairs two at a time, eager to escape the stairwell's foetid stench and a stoned teenage boy who attempted to bar his ascent. On reaching the third floor Peter went straight to number 12 and rang the doorbell. Loud drum and bass music emanated from the flat opposite. He waited until he could hear the teenager stumbling up the third floor stairs, then reached into the letterbox with one hand and fished about until his fingers connected with a key on the end of a piece of string.

The flat looked just as untidy, but this time had an extra air of neglect and aroma of decay. Peter picked up a pile of mail from a stained welcome mat, then kicked a few empty beer cans further along the hallway. He checked the electric meter at the end of the hall, added a few pounds to it, then flooded the kitchen with light.

The remains of his brother's last meal, mouldy and infested with maggots, still sat on the kitchen table. Empty wine bottles, beer cans and take-away boxes lay scattered over every worktop. The rubbish bin overflowed, and in the middle of the kitchen floor a rat sat up on its haunches and regarded him with interest. Peter ran towards the rat, picked it up by its tail, then opened a window and threw it outside. The bedroom held two single beds and a large wardrobe. One bed had not been used, but the other one contained stained sheets and dried vomit. He made a quick inspection of the other rooms, all in a similar state of chaos, and decided it was time to clean up, shut up, and make the best of a bad job.

CHAPTER ELEVEN

Mavis picked up her pay-as-you-go mobile phone and tapped in Peter's new number.

"Peter?"

"Hello Mum."

"Where *are* you?" Mavis' relief was palpable. "I've tried more than a few times."

"I've been cleaning up Phil's flat. The bloody state of it… you wouldn't believe."

"Where is he? Is he there?"

"No. I expect he's in hospital or rehab. You know what he's like."

"Have you got the … you know?"

"The goods? I sure have. Have you gone back to see Billy yet?"

"No … I'm doing as we planned. I'm waiting for him to come to *me*."

"Well, give him another day or so and then knock on the door and apologise. Don't let him get away."

"I don't intend to, Petey, it's not every day you meet a man who's won the lottery."

"Have the police been?"

"Yes. Billy's obviously told them about you, but all I said was that you'd been at the party the whole time and that currently I didn't know where you were. Well, I didn't up 'till now. They want to speak to you. They searched my flat and they might go to yours, but I *know* they'll take fingerprints in Billy's bedroom."

"I was careful, don't worry. They won't find anything. I'm going to lie low here for a while and sit on the beach."

"Keep the goods there. Don't open any bank accounts. Spend your bit in dribs and drabs, not all at once. Sift through Phil's mail to make sure the rent's not overdue… hopefully he pays it by standing order from his housing benefit. Don't forget to pay the rent on your own place as well, but don't splash any money about. Only use your new phone now, and I hope you've got rid of the other one? After a while I'll come down on the train and pick up my half, but it'll be a while before I can do that, maybe about six months or so."

"Okay. I'll wait to hear from you. Yeah, I ditched the other phone. 'Bye for now."

Mavis ended the call and wondered for the thousandth time why she'd had to wait until she had almost set one foot in the grave before her life could take a sudden upturn. Colin had drank away the majority of his wages for their entire married life, and had left her nothing but debts and empty vodka bottles to prove he had once been a living, breathing pig of a man. She was entitled to some happiness, the same as everybody else, and now with her new husband-to-be's money she was going to grab happiness by the throat before it once more dissipated into the ether.

A knock on her front door brought Mavis out of her reverie. She looked through her spy-hole to see Billy's daughter staring in her direction. She liked Joy the least out of all three of them. She jumped back from the spy-hole in alarm and opened the door.

"Hello, Joy. What can I do for you?"

"I want to find out what you know about Dad's money going missing, and also why you aren't helping him in his hour of need."

"He's accused my son of stealing it. I was angry with him because he's got no proof. It could have been anybody."

Mavis kept eye contact with Joy, and decided to let the woman stand out in the communal corridor.

"Can I come in?" Joy looked up and down the passageway. "It's better to discuss something like this without all the neighbours listening behind closed doors."

"There's nothing to discuss, Joy. The police have finished with me. Yes, Peter hasn't got a job and is on benefits, but that doesn't mean he's dishonest."

"Do you have another son?"

"Not any more." Mavis shook her head. "He died... alcoholism."

"Sorry."

"Yeah... well.. . all water under the bridge now. Can I help with anything else?"

"No. My sister, brother and myself are trying to get to the bottom of all this."

"Good luck."

"Perhaps go and cheer Dad up. He's down in the dumps."

"I will. I've calmed down now. I'll go along later when I've had my lunch and Billy's had his nap. Goodbye for now."

Mavis's heart raced as she closed the door.

***

There was a dejected look about him. Mavis gave Billy a sheepish grin.

"Sorry to fly off the handle like that. A mother always sticks up for her children, whatever their age. Do you forgive me?"

"I suppose so." Billy opened his door wider. "Come in. Where is he now? The police want to interview him."

"I saw him at your party for the first time in two years. He's a grown man and I have no idea where he goes." Mavis stepped over the threshold. "To my knowledge he's never been in trouble with the police before. He's just one of life's free spirits."

"*Freeloading* spirits, you mean?" Billy hobbled towards the front room. "Living off taxpayers' money?"

"Let's not start another argument. I've brought a couple of cream cakes with me as a peace offering. Shall I put the kettle on?"

"If you like." Billy sat down heavily in his armchair. "I can't bear the thought that somebody's been snooping around in my flat."

"Did they take anything else?" Mavis handed Billy the bag of eclairs. "I'll get two plates."

"Don't think so. They went straight for the money. I wonder if they knew it was there, or if they just found it on the off-chance?"

"How would anybody know it was there? Did you tell anyone?"

"No, of course not." Billy shook his head. "I'm old, but I'm not stupid."

Mavis went into Billy's kitchen, switched the kettle on, then silently opened and closed various drawers and cupboards to peep inside. When the tea had brewed she carried a tray containing two steaming mugs and two small plates into the living room.

"Here you are. Tea's up. There's a plate here for your éclair."

"Too late. I've already eaten it."

The same thing had always happened with Colin; no finesse. Slurping left over milk from a Weetabix breakfast straight from the bowl. No cure for his addictions either, but that was another story.

CHAPTER TWELVE

Andrew Perkins flexed his knuckles and watched Mavis oozing charm in his father's direction. He found it somewhat difficult to control a powerful build-up of irritation.

"So you want *me* to take the two of you shopping in town on Saturday so you can buy an engagement ring?

"Well, yes, if that's possible, as we would both like to choose it. Ann has a wheelchair in storage that we can use." Mavis cooed. "You see, I'm not strong enough to cope with getting Billy in and out of the car, and I'm worried in case he might fall over. I can't pick him up if he does."

Andrew dug his thumbnail hard into his forefinger.

But you can pick his money up.

"Is that okay with *you*, Dad?"

"Whatever Mavis wants." Billy sent a semblance of a smile in Mavis's direction. "We'll have to go to the bank first so that I can get some more money out."

"Don't get loads out and put it in another box." Andrew regarded the expression on Mavis's face as he spoke. "Look at what happened when you *did*."

"Andy, I've learned my lesson. Don't keep going on about it."

"So that's settled then?" Mavis turned her gaze towards Andrew. "Saturday at, shall we say, ten o'clock? Maybe we can have lunch as well, so that I can get to know you better."

"No can do." Andrew shook his head. "Mal's got football in the afternoon and I have to give him a lift."

"Shame. Oh well, Billy and I can find something to do in the afternoon."

Andrew quickly dowsed virtual cold water on the thought of Mavis and his father in bed. The woman put hackles up the back of his neck, and he couldn't quite put his finger on why.

***

His father had definitely become less mobile. Andrew steadied Billy's feeble frame as he eased the old man into the front seat of his car. There was time to ask the one question he had been itching to ask while Mavis took a few moments to visit the lavatory.

"Are you still certain you want to go through with the marriage, Dad?"

"Of course." Billy winced with pain as he lifted his legs into the car. "How did *you* feel when you were engaged to Lesley?"

"Sexually frustrated." Andrew laughed. "She wanted the ring on her finger first."

"I'm of sound mind, I love Mavis, and I want her companionship. Sex is a bonus, but at my age it'll be nice not to be on my own anymore."

"You don't have to get married to have Mavis's company, Dad. You've got it already. You need to make sure she's not just after your winnings."

"She doesn't know about the lottery win. I want to get married because that's what you do when you love somebody, *and* it'll stop all the wagging tongues."

"Have you got your bank card?"

"Yes, it's in my wallet."

Out of the corner of his eye Andrew could see the object of their discussion striding towards him. Mavis climbed into the back, with an audible sigh.

"Okay, Mavis?"

"Of course." Mavis nodded. "Just not a lot of leg room."

"Move over behind *my* seat then, as I've had to push Dad's seat back to make it easier for him to get in."

Mavis's head was now blocking the view from his rear window. Andrew gave a quick glance in the mirror and caught Mavis staring at him quite intensely. He felt hairs rise on the back of his neck as he started the engine and pulled away from the kerb.

They travelled some distance in silence. Within 15 minutes Andrew heard snores emanating from his left and tapping from behind. He chanced a glimpse in the mirror at the back seat, where Mavis stared down at her phone.

"Messaging somebody?" Andrew stopped at a red light.

"I might be."

Rhythmic tapping of her long fingernails on the mobile phone irritated him. Andrew turned into a multi-storey and parked the car in a disabled space on the second floor.

"Come on, Dad, wake up." Andrew gave Billy a shake. "Time to buy an engagement ring."

"I wasn't asleep."

"Is that so?" Andrew took his father's blue parking badge and put it on the dashboard, then stepped out of the car and fetched a wheelchair from the boot. "You could have fooled me."

"I heard you asking Mavis whether she was sending a message to somebody."

"My sister, Billy. I sent a message to Edith to let her know where we were going." Mavis climbed out of the car. "That's all."

"I didn't know you had a sister." Billy flopped down into the wheelchair. "Where does she live?"

"Bembridge, on the Isle of Wight."

"So that's why you want to move there?" Andrew locked the car and grabbed the wheelchair's handles.

"Could be."

The woman's evasiveness grated on his nerves. Andrew picked up speed through the car park, causing Mavis to pant as she half-ran/ half-walked to keep up.

"Slow down.. it's not a route march."

"Sorry." Andrew manoeuvred the wheelchair through a door leading to the lift area. "It's my normal pace."

"Well, it's not *mine*."

He heard her phone ping in the lift. She turned the display screen away from him as she answered the message. Andrew decided he really did not like Mavis at all. When they arrived at the bank he pointed to a bench outside.

"Sit there and recover from the route march. We won't be a minute."

He could tell she was about to protest, but had then thought again. He pushed the wheelchair into the bank and joined the queue to the counter. The further Mavis stayed away from his father's bank account, the better he would like it.

CHAPTER THIRTEEN

Taking care not to mark the freshly painted front door, Peter turned the key and unlocked his brother's flat. He stepped into the hallway and a pleasant tang of air freshener assailed his nostrils. Notwithstanding the vandalised main lobby, the flats themselves were well laid out and spacious. He walked into the living area and a feeling of satisfaction washed over him as he glanced around at the results of his labours. Gone were the mould-encrusted plates of takeaway food, empty beer cans and overflowing ashtrays. The carpet had been shampooed and vacuumed, the curtains washed and re-hung, and the settee and armchairs brushed and covered with attractive throws. The bedroom boasted two pristine beds with new matching duvet covers and pillowcases. He had hated cleaning up his brother's mess, but with around £40,000 pounds on the premises he could not trust a local team of housekeepers.

He backtracked to the kitchen; not one saucepan, cup or plate was out of place. In Phil's bedroom he opened the wardrobe and checked his stash of money still sat on the lower shelf in a gym bag where he had last left it. Anxious to splash out and spend the lot, he quickly closed the wardrobe door and exited the room lest temptation got the better of him.

Weatherwise they were slowly edging towards summer. Phil's flat had become quite hot sometimes, and the days had finally warmed up enough to sit on the beach and cast an eye on girls wearing not too much at all. Peter looked out of the kitchen window at the vast expanse of beach opposite, and decided to invest in a few pairs of shorts and some new tee shirts. His rent still went out on standing order, and various benefits had piled up nicely as he had long ago decided to live in a frugal style. Determined not to get to know any neighbours and keep himself to himself, he always made sure the landing was empty before running to the access stairs and scuttling down. The last time he had seen his brother he was surprised at how much they resembled each other now that both had lost some hair and had grown beards to compensate. Hopefully any neighbours might think Phil was still in residence.

The long-awaited call from his mother came one evening as he settled down to watch a football match on TV. Peter picked up his phone and accepted the call.

"Hi."

"You'd better get the train down tomorrow and meet *me* somewhere instead. Billy and his children might all be suspicious if I'm gone for too long. Bring my half of the goods. Don't come to the flats. I'll say I'm going shopping, then I can meet you at Epsom and we can go to the bank together. Every bank I tried wanted you to be present, so I've booked an appointment with Lloyds. It's not too far away, but nobody knows me at Epsom. Get a train there and wait for me outside Superdrug about one o'clock."

"Okay."

Peter ended the call then settled down to watch the match.

***

He looked in vain for a wedding ring on the third finger of her left hand.

"You and Billy not married yet?" Peter walked with his mother towards Lloyds Bank in Epsom's busy shopping centre. "I thought you would have organised it by now."

"I did, but it had to be postponed." Mavis panted. "He caught Covid and he's only just getting over it. He must have got it when we went to buy the engagement ring."

"Christ, that could have been serious." Peter turned to look at Mavis. "Try and keep him alive for a while longer."

"The wedding is set for three months' time. The hotel is booked up 'til then."

"I can't wait to do a bit of shopping. "Peter glanced around."I've given myself two hundred quid to spend. I'll go back later on the train and have a pint on the way back to the flat to celebrate our good fortune."

"The police don't seem to be too bothered now, and Billy's kids have given up worrying about where the money went. They're around more now though, it's a nuisance. Billy's getting more forgetful. Even the grandchildren come snooping round. Between the lot of them they hardly leave him alone for more than one day. I *know* they don't like me."

"They'd like you even less if they knew what you're really up to."

"I think they already know… that's why they don't leave him alone."

"They can't stop the wedding, Mum, just as long as he still wants to get married."

"Oh he does." Mavis nodded. "Anyway, I'll make sure he does."

CHAPTER FOURTEEN

Phil Renshaw closed his eyes momentarily against the hot sun on his face, and felt good for the first time in at least a year. The agonising stomach cramps, nausea and shakes had at last left him, along with what could only be regarded as a savage craving for alcohol. He turned to the left, where Jack, Charge Nurse extraordinaire, held out one hand.

"Good luck, Phil. I mean it in the nicest possible way when I tell you I don't want to see you here ever again."

"Thanks for everything you've done for me." Phil shook Jack's hand. "I don't know if I could have made it through Rehab without you."

"My pleasure. Now piss off."

Phil laughed, gave Jack one last wave, then made his way to the train station. He tried to remember what state he might have left his flat in when he'd decided enough was enough, but could not recall anything much that had happened in the previous year.

The train ride to Margate took only half an hour. Phil felt comforted at familiar scenery as he left Margate station and walked towards the seafront. He stood for a while next to the statue of a lifeboatman looking out to sea, and enjoyed the cool breeze on his face. Invigorated and ready to tackle his shambles of a flat, Phil turned on his heel then ran across the road towards the tower block he had called home for the past ten years. Disappointed at how the main lobby had deteriorated even further in the time he'd been away, he took the stairs two at a time to the third floor and then stopped short.

The door to number 12 had obviously just recently had a coat of paint. Puzzled, Phil reached through the letterbox, found the key, and let himself into his flat. An unfamiliar aroma of air freshener filled the air. The hallway furniture was just as he'd remembered, but the carpet had been vacuumed and he could not see even a speck of dirt.

Phil crept further into the flat and inspected each room in turn. The kitchen appeared spotless, as did the living area. He moved into the bedroom; the beds had duvet covers on and matching pillowcases that he did not recognise at all. He opened his wardrobe; his clothes had all been folded up and laid on the bottom, and somebody else's trousers and shirts hung where his clothes had once been.

A stranger had moved into his flat and was sleeping in his bed! He delved further into the wardrobe; a gym bag on the lower shelf contained what he surmised was thousands of pounds. Phil stepped back in alarm. The council had obviously re-let the flat while he'd been away, even though his rent had continued to be paid. What the fuck had they been thinking of? Now he was homeless, that was for sure. Okay, he would have the last laugh. He would take the gym bag, which doubtless contained enough money to enable him to rent a hotel for a couple of nights, and then as soon as possible would visit the council offices and sort out some new accommodation.

He opened the top drawer of his chest of drawers; his pair of gloves were still there, and Phil put them on. A trendy leather jacket hung on a hanger in the wardrobe. Phil donned the jacket, picked up the gym bag, and had a quick look around for anything else of the bastard's worth taking. In the kitchen he found a lasagna in the fridge. He warmed it up in the microwave and wolfed it down together with a pint of milk. Now the bloke who had moved into his flat would have no dinner that evening. Serve him right.

Outside it was too hot for the leather jacket, but Phil kept it on even though he had begun to sweat by the time he had walked around the corner to the Premier Inn. He needed to gather his thoughts, and the nearby Premier Inn was the most convenient for an overnight stay. He would even be able to eat out later on in The Promenade bar/restaurant next door, a luxury he had not enjoyed for some time.

***

Phil, his wallet now fifty pounds richer, walked through the Premier Inn's main corridor towards the side door of The Promenade bar. The usual summer sun seekers thronged the bar at the end of the day, and their fractious children, stained and sandy from the beach, whined for food. Phil ordered a chicken salad and an orange juice, and took a corner seat away from a particularly obnoxious mother and three badly behaved boys. He sat back in his chair, and while awaiting his order surreptitiously checked out his fellow diners. An elderly couple ate in silence on the next table, two twentysomethings held hands and gazed into each other's eyes, and a lone diner facing away from him shovelled chips into his mouth in a mechanical fashion as he read a newspaper propped up in front of him.

Phil focused on the man. Something about the back of his head seemed familiar, especially when he cleared his throat the way his brother used to. Phil stood up, walked over to the man's table, and took a good long look at the face that was so like his own.

"Pete? Bloody hell, it *is* you, isn't it?" Phil ignored the startled but guarded expression on his brother's face. "What the fuck are you doing here?"

"Eating my dinner." Peter speared another chip with his fork. "What does it *look* like?"

"I haven't seen you in years. Do you live in Margate as well?"

"I only moved here recently. I've just got off the train. I went to see Mum today. Where are you living now?"

"Well, I've just got out of rehab. I rolled up at my old flat earlier on, but I think the council must have re-let it. I'm going to the council offices tomorrow and have a go at them. The buggers have still been taking the rent from my housing benefit."

"You've been inside the flat?"

"Yeah." Phil sat down opposite his brother and let out a wry laugh. "Whoever's got it now must have spent hours tidying it up."

"*I* did, you bastard. It was a pig sty."

Phil held his surprise in check and waved to a waitress carrying a loaded tray.

"Over here, darlin', I've changed tables." He picked up a knife and fork. "Ta."

The waitress moved away and Phil ate with relish while ignoring Peter's stare.

"If I know you at all, I expect you've now picked up the bag that I left in the wardrobe."

"*My* wardrobe." Phil chewed thoughtfully. "*My* flat. *My* bag."

"Where is it?" Peter looked under the table. "Where's my bag?"

"And I know *you*, you bastard. "Phil chuckled. "You're lying low. That's someone else's money, isn't it?"

"Might be." Peter sunk half a pint of beer in one go. "Okay, you can have half if you tell me where it is."

"In my room here." Phil poured salad cream on his plate. "I thought I was homeless. I'll eat this, oh, and I ate your lasagna by the way, then you can come back to the flat and tell me all about what's been going on. Anyway, you might have asked me if you could take over my place."

"You weren't there and I didn't have a choice. I'm asking *now*. Let me stay and you'll find out there's more where that lot came from."

"It's a deal." Phil put down his knife and held out his hand. "Shake on it, bro."

A reluctant handshake confirmed the deal. Phil finished the rest of his salad in silence

CHAPTER FIFTEEN

"Who is Queen, Mister Perkins?"

"Elizabeth the Second." Billy regarded the doctor with disdain. "Everyone knows that."

"That question was a bit tricky. Actually it's Queen Camilla now, Dad." Andrew sighed. "She's married to King Charles."

"No she's not." Billy shook his head. "Charlie's married to Princess Diana."

"Mister Perkins, I'm going to give you an address to remember, and I'll ask you to repeat it in a while." Doctor Trent consulted his notes. "Forty two West Street. Remember that, but for now please can you tell me who the Prime Minister is."

"Don't *you* know, then?" Billy, impatient, drummed his fingers on the table in front of him.

"I've forgotten. You need to remind me."

"It's Tony Blair." Billy laughed. "And all the while I thought *I* was the one going mad."

"What was that address I just gave you?"

"You haven't said any address. My son can back me up on that one."

"Do you remember forty two West Street?" Andrew spoke gently into his father's ear.

"Who lives there?" Billy shrugged. "*I* don't."

"Where *do* you live then?" Doctor Trent jotted down a few notes. "What's *your* address?"

"I live in Regent's Park Zoo with the reptiles."

"Have a seat outside in the waiting room, Mister Perkins, just for a minute or two."

Billy got to his feet with difficulty. He had forgotten exactly where the waiting room was. Reassured to feel Andrew's hand guiding him, he allowed himself to be led to a seat. He must have dozed, as the next thing he knew Andrew had shaken him awake.

"Come on, Dad, let's go back to the car."

Where was he? Billy had no idea. Life had become very confusing. When Andrew stopped the car he saw two women edging forward towards him, one younger and one older. He didn't recognise either one.

"Who are they?" Billy looked out of the car window. "Why are they staring at me?"

"The one on the left is Joy, your daughter, and the other one is Mavis."

"Who's Mavis?" Billy felt like poking his tongue out at them.

"You're engaged to be married to her."

"I'm bloody well not!" Billy cringed further away from the window. "I'm not getting married again at my age!"

"Tell *her* that." Andrew leaned over and opened the passenger door. "Tell her, so that we've got it on record, so to speak."

"Only too happy to." Billy swung both legs around and put his feet on the floor. "Piss off, the pair of you!"

"Now, now, Billy, that's not very nice. We're getting married next week."

"I don't think so." Joy shook her head. "Mavis, you can see he's not in his right mind anymore. I and my brother and sister will be seeking a solicitor so that Dad can make a will."

"Of course I'm in my right fucking mind!" Billy shouted as loudly as he could. "I don't want to get married. All I want is my lunch."

"You need to cancel the wedding, Mavis. Dad has been diagnosed with early dementia. If you don't cancel it, then *I* will." Andrew put Billy's walking frame in front of him. "Leave us alone to look after our father. He's not marrying anybody."

For some unknown reason Billy felt sorry for the older woman, who hurried away with tears in her eyes. He wished they'd *all* leave him alone so that he could try and sort his mind out.

***

"Dad, this is Ewan Meekings, he's a solicitor. He's come to see you." Andrew spoke close to his father's ear. "Joy and Amber are here too."

Billy looked up from his armchair at a middle aged man with grey hair, who wore a grey suit coupled with a bright red tie.

"I don't want to see any solicitor."

"Mister Perkins, just call me Ewan. I'm here to help you make a will. Your children called me."

"I haven't got any children."

"Dad, don't be silly. I'm Andrew. Don't you recognise me?"

Billy was hungry and wished everyone would go away. He had no idea who anybody was, let alone this man who kept calling him *Dad.*

The red tie spoke to the other man. Billy heard the words *Court of Protection* and *Power of Attorney*. He wondered if it was macaroni cheese for lunch again.

EPILOGUE

Peter accepted his mother's incoming call whilst identifying as a Jack Lemmon character telling his Walter Matthau-like brother to take his feet off his own coffee table.

"Hi, Mum."

"The wedding's off, Pete. Billy's been diagnosed with dementia. He's gone downhill fast. He's raving."

"So what happens now?" Peter sat up straight, aware of Phil's sudden interest.

"I've found out from the warden that his children are going to the Court of Protection to gain Power of Attorney. Billy's going to be moved into a care home when there's a bed available. I know the police still want to speak to you about the missing money."

"So there won't be any more?"

"Only the money you got from his room."

"Shit. Phil's back now. He's let me stay with him, and I've given him half my share."

"Is he sober?"

"Seems to be."

"Oh well, I'm glad he's okay and that you're both together again. I don't think I need to speak to him. He said some downright cruel words to me the last time we had a conversation."

"He probably doesn't remember." Mindful of his brother's proximity, Peter chose his words carefully. "You know how it is."

"No I don't, and I never will. More importantly, what are you going to do about the police?"

"Oh… see out the summer here, then turn up at my flat and deny everything. I haven't withdrawn any money from my old bank account yet, so they won't be able to find out where I am in the meantime. It'll all die down soon enough."

"That money won't stretch for long."

"I know, but as they say… it'll be good while it lasts. We'll have the best summer we've ever had."

"Good luck to you, son."

"'Bye for now."

Peter ended the call and turned to his brother.

"Get your feet off the table. I've not long polished it."

THE END

TRIO

THE JOURNEY

CHAPTER ONE

"Before you go on holiday I want you to arrange my funeral."

My mother Beryl had been on at me for ages to do this, but so far I'd managed to put it off.

"Why? Are you going to pop your clogs then?"

"I will soon, and you know it. All my friends have pre-paid funeral plans, except me."

"Well, it's not a pre-requisite just because you're a pensioner and live in sheltered housing."

"Just do it." Beryl replied with much force. "I'm ready to go whenever the good Lord feels free to take me."

I had to admit, I'd never arranged a funeral before for somebody who was still alive. I drove into town and had a look around to see which undertakers' parlours I liked the look of. There were three to choose from, and I picked one with two pristine white tombstones in the shop window sitting atop a thick black velvet cloth adorned with fresh lilies, and with four well-polished limousines and a hearse parked down a private side alley. *Business must be piling up.*

Taking a deep breath I opened the door and walked inside; it was quiet as the grave, so to speak. Suddenly a man appeared out of nowhere, dressed in a black three piece suit, black tie and white shirt.

"Good morning. May I help you?"

He was unsmiling, but somehow unctuous. I felt rather out of my depth, but carried on.

"Er…I know this is going to sound silly, but can I arrange a funeral for somebody who is still alive please?"

"Of course!" The man replied with a smile as though the situation happened every day. "My name is Ben Collins. Please call me Ben and come this way. What you need is the Dignity in Dying pre-paid plan."

What the hell is dignified about death? I was led into a back room where piped music played very softly. A large table and ten chairs filled up most of the space. Ben pulled out a chair for me.

"Would you like a cup of tea?"

"Yes please."

He disappeared briefly before returning with a cup of hot but anaemic-looking liquid, which he placed carefully on the table. He then took down a folder from a shelf and seated himself opposite.

"Now then; who are you arranging the funeral for?"

"My mother, Mrs Beryl Taylor."

"Cremation or burial?"

"She hasn't said. I think she wants to be surprised."

I could not begin to tell you how strange it was to speak to an undertaker about somebody who was still very much alive.

"Date of birth?"

"Twenty first of January, nineteen twenty eight."

"And where is Mrs Taylor living?"

I gave Ben my mother's address and my own contact details. He stopped writing and pushed some pamphlets towards me.

"Have you given any thought to what kind of coffin you would like?"

To be quite honest, whether to lay Beryl out in pine, teak, oak, wicker or cardboard had never crossed my mind.

"Er…no, I'm afraid."

"Well, we don't have to worry too much about that at the moment."

What a relief. Ben skipped on down.

"Would you like no car, one car, or more than one?"

Beryl only had a few friends, as the majority had either all died or were not particularly well. There remained only family members.

"I think two will be enough."

"That's settled then!" Ben looked uncomfortable. "There just remains the small matter of payment."

"Ah yes." Beryl had given me total control over her finances some time back, and I produced a blank cheque from mine and Mum's joint account. "How much will it be?"

"Prices will be fixed until November, and will then rise substantially. You have done well to sign up now."

I waited patiently in case Ben wanted to give me some more old flannel.

"That will be four thousand six hundred and fifty pounds for a cremation. A burial will be more expensive."

I nearly fell off my chair. Dad's burial costs were only £250 in 1977. No wonder undertakers never seem to go out of business.

"Good God!" I could not help the exclamation.

"Costs rise each year I'm afraid. With the 'Dignity in Dying' plan you'll find all other establishments in the area are the same price."

What a surprise!

"Well, we'd best have a cremation then."

Ben swiftly pocketed the cheque from my trembling fingers, and Beryl's wish was granted. Her swift passage into the hereafter was assured, and now we could all rest in peace.

CHAPTER TWO

Arranging Mum's funeral had put a bit of a damper on my holiday. I sat on the cruise ship's decking with Sam as the ship made its way to Costa Maya, but all I could think about was Mum lying dead in a coffin. She had kissed me goodbye with more warmth than usual on the night before our departure, and although she was healthy enough for somebody in their nineties, I had known for quite a while that of course she could depart this life at any time. Granted, she couldn't wait to be free of arthritic pain, but I knew her days were full with various clubs and hobbies and to me she seemed to be enjoying her dotage.

All the countries we visited on that Caribbean cruise were too hot for me. After a week I wanted to go home to good old Blighty, and I tended to stay in the air-conditioned comfort of the ship when it docked at a port. If Mum had been computer literate I could have visited the Wi-Fi room on board and sent her an email, but electronic messages, texts and social media were far beyond her comprehension.

Our son had the job of visiting Mum while we were away. He sent daily updates by text, and mentioned how she seemed more confused that when he'd last seen her. I realised that due to work commitments he had not contacted his grandmother for over two months, and so any decline would be more pronounced. Was Beryl deteriorating into the early stages of Alzheimer's disease? I'd seen my mother every day for a few years now, and to me she always seemed rather batty; she had stuffed piles of toilet rolls and incontinence pads in her storage cupboard but would still send me out to buy more. The epidemic of dysentery she was well prepared for had so far refused to arrive.

To be honest it was a relief to get home. I had felt too guilty to enjoy our time away while still thinking that Mum might die at any moment. I had kept my thoughts from Sam and had taken part in on-board activities, but as soon as I could I drove to Mum's sheltered housing complex. There she sat with her cronies in the community hall, drinking tea and bitching about Mrs So-and-So who preferred to keep herself to herself. To be honest, I didn't blame Mrs So-and-So at all.

"Where have you been? It's not like you to stay away so long."

"I already told you, Mum. Sam and I went on a cruise."

"Well, it's all right for some, isn't it?"

"We talked about it the last time I was here. Don't you remember?"

"We did nothing of the kind. I thought you'd forgotten all about me."

"Leon came round to see you instead, didn't he?"

"No, he didn't. I haven't seen him in years."

Mum's behaviour was strange, as she didn't seem to be in her right mind. I'd only been away for a fortnight, but I could see why Leon thought she had gone downhill somewhat. Happily, the following day she seemed more like her usual self, and asked me whether I'd had a good time on the cruise. I lied and said I'd had the best time ever.

TRIO

CHAPTER THREE

Beryl finally found herself in the River Styx's waiting room about two years later after the ravages of Alzheimer's disease had taken away her entire personality. Immediate and extended family stood around her bed as she paid Charon his fee with a beatific smile on her face. As he rowed her across I saw my mother's spirit leave her body, although nobody else in the room did. My grandfather appeared, a younger man than I recognised, to help his daughter into the afterlife.

There was nothing else to do except to contact Ben and arrange for Mum's shell to be cremated. When younger she had often instructed me to stick a pin in her body to ensure death had taken place, but after the doctor had been to certify there was no sign of life I soon decided that particularly onerous task did not need to be carried out.

I visited Mum one morning in the undertakers' parlour after Ben and his pals had finished doing whatever they do with dead bodies. She looked very peaceful lying there, as though she was just asleep. Her hair had been washed and styled, but rather too much makeup had been slapped on her face. I suppose they wanted to give her a rosy complexion, but in my opinion they'd overdone it. She looked like she had been in the sun too long. Her hands had been placed on her chest, and a rosary strung between them.

As I sat there I reached out to touch one of her fingers, and received the shock of my life... it was soft and warm! I jumped out of the chair in alarm, backed up against the wall, and froze to the spot in terror. Mum continued to lie there unmoving, unassuming, and... warm. Suddenly she sat up in her coffin, looked over at me, and gave me a wink.

"Come back and sit with me. I've never hurt you, have I?"

"No." I squeaked. "You haven't."

"Well I'm not going to *now* either. Don't shout for anyone to come in. I just want to tell you what it's like in the next life."

I felt like sticking a pin in *myself* to prove I wasn't dreaming. For two and a half years Mum had only talked gibberish, and now all her words made perfect sense. With eyes fixed on Mum, I inched back to my chair. Mum looked surreal sitting up in her white shroud with that crimson face. The rosary had slipped from between her hands, and she twirled the beads around on one finger. I stared at her with my mouth wide open.

"Hurry up. I haven't got all day."

I didn't know whether to laugh or cry. I sat down and let out a shaky breath. Mum stopped twirling the rosary, propped her pillow up a bit, and leaned back.

"You'll never believe it, but I'm with my dad again now. Nan is here too, but that's another story. Dad's fine, and he's just as I remember him from when he was a young man. The two miscarriages I had turned out to be two girls, who have grown up to be beautiful women. You've got two sisters, Stevie… imagine that!"

"I can't imagine it, Mum." I shook my head. "It's all too much to think about."

"That's another thing, Stevie, all you have to do is *think* about a place you want to go to, and you're there straight away by the power of thought."

"Bloody hell." I relaxed a bit, kept my voice down as much as I could, and wondered whether I should take a photo of my mother with my mobile phone."

"You can…" Mum shrugged. "But it won't come out. Yeah, I can read your thoughts as well."

"Is nothing sacred?" I took my phone from my bag and held it up. "Smile!"

Mum's features contorted into a grimace. She pushed back a tuft of grey hair from her forehead, which promptly fell out onto the shroud.

"Oops, clumsy…" Mum sighed. "Never mind. It had gone a bit thin by the end anyway."

I tapped the photo icon on my phone, but all the latest picture showed was my dead mother lying motionless in her coffin with rosary beads in her hands.

"Told you." Mum smirked at me.

"What do you do all day?" I could hardly believe the conversation which was taking place.

"There is no night or day, Stevie. There's a beautiful garden with colours and flowers that you've never seen or could identify. I can't even begin to describe the music you can hear in the garden. Anyone you've ever loved is right there with you. There's some kind of being as well, but I've not seen it as yet."

"You mean *God*?"

"Don't know. I haven't been here long enough. I'm just having a ball floating around without any pain at the moment. I've even been back to my grandmother's old house in Inverness. Isn't that strange? She was there to greet me in the doorway, even though she had passed thirty years before *I* did."

"Strange isn't the word for it." I rubbed my eyes, opened them again, and Mum still smiled at me. "I hope nobody's watching me in here. They'll send for a man who carries one of those jackets that do up at the back."

"No, you're all right. You just have to get used to the fact that we don't actually die. Well, our bodies do, but our spirits don't. I'm glad I've got shot of that old, worn out body at last. I feel about twenty five years old again."

I tried again to take another photograph and even a video to prove Mum's confirmation of life after death. Both were unsuccessful.

CHAPTER FOUR

The door to the viewing room opened a little, and Ben's head appeared in the doorway.

"Would you like a cup of tea? There's a machine in the other room."

"Yes please." I turned to Mum, who had draped one arm over the side of the coffin. "No sugar, thanks."

"Right-o. Coming up."

Ben disappeared down the corridor, and Mum let out a throaty laugh.

"Don't worry. He just sees an old dead lady lying here …he even embalmed me a few days ago. You've got second sight, which I think must have been passed down from your grandmother. It comes in handy at times like these."

"You reckon?"

My heart had returned to its natural 60ish beats per minute. In fact I was actually enjoying myself. I crossed one leg over the other and relaxed into my seat.

"Tell me what else goes on in the next world before he comes back."

"Well…" Mum rested her head on one hand. "We can be reincarnated if we want to, in order to put right our mistakes and move further along the spiritual path. I might do this, but right now I'm enjoying visiting all the places and people which have good memories for me. One of these days I'm going to come back as a robin and sit on your window ledge."

"I can give you some mouldy bread to eat."

"Your kindness knows no bounds."

Footsteps along the corridor let me know that Ben had returned with my drink. Other than thanking him, I remained silent while he handed me a mug of tea. After he had tactfully left me alone, I turned again to my mother, who looked remarkably well as she sat up straighter in her coffin.

"What happens when you get to the end of the spiritual path?" I took a sip of tea. "Where can you go when you can't travel any further?"

"They say you reach Nirvana. Don't ask me what it's like or where it is, because I haven't been there yet."

"Is God there?"

"Maybe... maybe not. Perhaps it depends on your spiritual state."

"What mistakes have you got to put right, Mum?"

"They tell you when you want to know. I don't think I can face it at the moment."

"*Who* tells you?"

"Those who've reached Nirvana. They let you know what you need to do, and then put you back on Earth. Sometimes you have to have many incarnations before you're spiritually pure."

"Blimey." I took a large swig of tea. "So murderers and the like might never get there?"

"True." Mum nodded. "Or it could take many, many lifetimes. I'm learning all the time, but sooner or later you have to face your demons."

"You were a good mum to me, apart from the last two years when, to be honest, you weren't all there. I haven't got any complaints, even though you didn't recognise me at the end."

"That's so sweet, but I've got to come to terms with the relationship I had with your grandmother. I was awful to her. There was never much love lost between us, and although I know she's around me, I haven't yet spoken to her. Dad helped me over to the Spirit world because of the strong love link I had with him that I didn't have with Mum. He looked after your sisters when they came over here. Like I said, I've got to face my demons before I can move on."

"You'd better hurry up then, otherwise I might overtake you on the road."

"You may well do, Stevie. I've got to do things in my own time, but now my energy levels are falling. Come back and sit with me tomorrow."

I finished my tea and Mum disappeared, leaving me with just her empty shell again. Ben tapped lightly on the door and then opened it.

"Everything okay? We will be closing in ten minutes' time. Do you want to come back tomorrow?"

"Yes please."

I looked at my watch; several hours had passed since I had arrived. I had missed lunch, and suddenly felt famished. I had no idea where all the lost time had gone. I took one last look at Mum, and noticed the grey tuft of hair she had pulled out was now resting on top of the rosary.

***

Not sure where Mum had disappeared to, but when I arrived at the viewing room the next day all I saw was her body lying there still and silent. Her hands fitted neatly together, and the rosary, bereft of any hair extension, had been placed once again between her fingers. I took a proffered cup of tea from Ben, and sat sipping it in the hope of a repeat performance from the day before. I waited until Ben had collected my empty cup before whispering.

"Mum?"

Just as I wondered whether I had dreamt the whole thing, my mother sat up and gave me a grin through two peculiarly red lips.

"Hi Stevie. You should have called me sooner. I was showing your sisters where we used to live. What have *you* been doing?"

"Sitting here looking at your dead body."

"Oh, that's not much fun, is it?" Mum laughed. "It's enough to drive you to drink."

"Well, I had a cup of tea, but nothing else. This is my last day, as it's your funeral tomorrow."

"Yes, I know. I'm not looking forward to finding out what goes on behind that curtain."

"You'll have to lie back and think of something pleasant."

"What are you going to do with my ashes?" Mum propped her elbow on the side of the coffin and rested her head on one hand.

"I've no idea as yet."

"Put them on Dad's grave, will you? No need to get the headstone changed. That'll be another expense you don't need."

"Well yes, I can do that, if that's what you want."

"Lovely, so that's settled." Mum smiled at me. "Love you, Stevie. Rest assured I'm not going to leave you."

"Love you too, Mum."

I left the funeral parlour on that second day much happier than I thought I'd ever be.

CHAPTER FIVE

The crowd waiting outside the crematorium mainly consisted of people I had never seen. I hadn't realised Mum had known so many people. I held Sam's hand as I followed behind the undertakers who carried Mum's coffin into the chapel. I hoped she appreciated the eulogy I had taken so much time and effort with.

I sat on the front bench with my family, sang the required hymns, and let my eyes roam around the chapel in the hope of seeing Mum. However, I think on that day she was too busy finding out what was going on behind the curtain to make an appearance. Disappointed, I filed outside with the others after the short service and made all the right murmurs when called upon to inspect the various floral tributes. I ate the ham salad and jelly and ice cream provided at the wake without really tasting it, and drank a large gin and tonic as I toasted the woman who had brought me into the world.

It was after the funeral that the reality sank in that my mother had gone. I found I missed our daily phone calls, even though sometimes I had barely concealed my irritation at being disturbed while watching TV or trying to work. Gregarious until Alzheimer's had dug its claws into her, my mother had always had enough jaw for ten rows of teeth (as my dad had once told me), but now her voice had been silenced.

I had to wait about 6 months after her death before I sensed her presence. My clothes in the wardrobe began to smell of her perfume, objects would go missing and then reappear, and lights and the TV would turn themselves on and off without human intervention. One cute little robin often sat on my window sill looking in at me as I ate my breakfast.

I woke up one night to find Mum sitting on the edge of my bed, still dressed in her shroud. I gave my husband a nudge:

"Sam... look..."

"Look at what?" Sam sat up. "It's the middle of the night."

"Mum's sitting on the bed. Can't you see her?"

"No." Sam laid back down on his pillow. "You're dreaming. I'm going back to sleep."

And he did. However, I did not. I continued to stare at my mother, whose features bore a benign, somehow saintly expression.

"It's lovely here, Stevie. You'll like it when you get here."

"I'm sure I will, but it's half past two in the morning."

"There's no time here."

"There *is* where *I* am." I yawned.

"Sorry. I'll go now, but don't be afraid of dying. There's nothing to it, and you'll go to a better place."

"It's the journey *getting* to the better place that bothers me."

"I'll be with you when it's *your* turn."

"Thanks a lot. That's a mighty comfort."

And somehow it was. Just before I fell asleep again I decided not to think about what might happen in the future and just live in the present. The journey to the other side would take place eventually, just as night follows day, but until it did I decided there was no use worrying about things that had not yet happened.

THE END

OTHER BOOKS BY STEVIE TURNER

A HOUSE WITHOUT WINDOWS
A LONG SLEEP
A RATHER UNUSUAL ROMANCE
ALYS IN HUNGERLAND
BARREN
CRUISING DANGER
EXAMINING KITCHEN CUPBOARDS
FALLING
FAREWELL
FINDING DAVID: A PARANORMAL SHORT STORY
FOR THE SAKE OF A CHILD
HIS LADYSHIP
LEG-LESS AND CHALAZA
LIFE: 18 SHORT STORIES
LILY: A SHORT STORY
MIND GAMES
NO SEX PLEASE, I'M MENOPAUSAL!
PARTNERS IN TIME
REPENT AT LEISURE
REVENGE
SCAM!
THE DAUGHTER-IN-LAW SYNDROME
THE DONOR
THE NOISE EFFECT
THE PILATES CLASS

www.ingramcontent.com/pod-product-compliance
Lightning Source LLC
Chambersburg PA
CBHW051952220626
47052CB00004B/907